D0374570

PHIL OF
CAMP CH-YO-CA

JOHN LUKE ROBERTSON

WITH TRAVIS THRASHER

TYNDALE HOUSE PUBLISHERS, INC., CAROL STREAM, IL

For manufacturing information regarding this product, please call 1-800-323-9400.

Library of Congress Cataloging-in-Publication Data

Robertson, John Luke, author.
    Phil & the ghost of Camp Ch-Yo-Ca / John Luke Robertson ; with Travis Thrasher.
        pages cm. — (Be your own duck commander ; [2])
    ISBN 978-1-4143-9814-3 (sc)
    I. Thrasher, Travis, 1971- author. II. Duck dynasty (Television program) III. Title.
IV. Title: Phil and the ghost of Camp Ch-Yo-Ca.
    PZ7.R5465Phi 2014
    [Fic]—dc23   2014024616

Printed in the United States of America

20   19   18   17   16   15   14
7   6   5   4   3   2   1

This book is dedicated to Papaw Phil.
Papaw, thank you for passing down your love of the outdoors
and adventure to me. Most important, thank you for
showing me that real men love God, value their families,
and support their country. You are a true hero.

WARNING!

DON'T READ THIS BOOK STRAIGHT THROUGH!

You'll miss out on all the fun if you do.

Instead, start at the beginning and decide where to go at the end of each chapter. This book is perfect for an evening around the campfire. There are lots of stories in it—some scary, others not so much. So grab some marshmallows and a chocolate bar (don't forget the graham crackers!) and follow the directions on which page number to go to at the end of each chapter. You'll be flipping around a lot, but that's part of the fun.

If your ghost story gets too scary, though, just start over at the beginning and choose a different path.

The great thing is, *you* are the main character. *You* make the decisions.

And right now, *you* get to be the *original* Duck Commander.

So put on your spider-stomping boots and get ready for a camping experience like no other.

Just make sure you don't meet up with a monster in the woods.

Also, you might want to avoid the lake late at night. There are strange things happening around there.

THIS IS WHO YOU ARE

Your name is Phil Alexander Robertson.

You are the first official Duck Commander. And it's true, you know. You really do command the ducks. With the help of some calls you invented that sound exactly like real ducks, as well as some blinds and guns.

You grew up in a log cabin near Vivian, a small

vii

town in rural Louisiana. You and your six brothers and sisters didn't have much in the way of luxuries. Money was scarce, so you hunted and fished and lived off the land to survive.

You are married to Miss Kay and have four grown boys: Alan, Jase, Willie, and Jep. Early on you decided to make a living off what you love: hunting and fishing. That's how you ended up creating the Duck Commander duck call and how a small family business took off.

You live in West Monroe, where the Duck Commander factory and business are currently located. You love your Lord and Savior Jesus Christ, your family, and hunting ducks. You believe hunting is your God-given, constitutional right to the pursuit of happiness. Hunting is what makes you happy, happy, happy.

You are about to embark on a very different kind of hunt. But you're ready.

You've always been ready for a great adventure.

THE GUEST

THERE'S NOTHING LIKE THE FEELING of sitting down in your favorite reclining chair on a Sunday night after eating Miss Kay's fried round steak with white sauce and then watching a little Jason Bourne. With your family around you, playing games in the background and laughing lots. That's really the definition of . . .

Yeah, you guessed it. *Happy, happy, happy.*

So when you hear a knock on the door that Sunday evening, you can't help but be curious. The family is all here, and none of them knock, anyway. The mean game of Egyptian Ratscrew going on at the dinner table pauses temporarily. Miss Kay answers and acts like she was expecting the guest.

Turns out it's Isaiah Bangs. Isaiah is the director over at Camp Ch-Yo-Ca, a popular Christian camp located in the piney woods of northern Louisiana near West Monroe. It's

1

a place where many campers have discovered Jesus. A place where many have also discovered love—like Willie and his wife, Korie, who met there when they were just kids. Isaiah is probably Willie's age, somewhere around forty. He's young at heart, and that's why the campers love him. He's got a big smile and big eyes to match. When he tells a ghost story, *everybody* listens.

You know Isaiah's a big talker, and it could take him up to half an hour just to make it the ten yards from the door to the couch by your chair. But tonight Isaiah heads straight for you. He must have something on his mind.

"Evenin', Phil."

You give him a nod. "Haven't seen you in a while. Busy summer at the camp?"

"Yes, sir. And that's why I called Miss Kay to ask if I could stop by."

You nod again and rub your bare feet together. "Did you eat?"

"Oh yes, thank you." Isaiah gives the younger kids a quick glance. "I was wonderin' if we could maybe talk outside."

"Sure thing." *What's up with him?*

As you slip on your shoes and head for the door, Isaiah hangs back at the kitchen table. "Hey, John Luke—you mind coming with your grandfather and me? Got something to discuss with you guys. About the camp."

John Luke stands up to follow you.

2

"Yeah, take him, 'cause he was winning," Willie says.

"I don't want to have to sit next to *Willie*," Jase shouts.

The joking and hollering continue while the three of you step into the fading light of the summer evening.

John Luke pulls out his smartphone in response to an annoying beep. You sigh. These new phones are like short leashes on overactive dogs.

While John Luke texts away, you head over to your shed to put some equipment away while Isaiah walks alongside, talking to you.

"They're going to be calling off this coming week of camp," he says.

You meet his eyes, surprised. "Since when? What's wrong?"

"We just made the decision. Counselors are calling parents, telling them not to bring their children. The kids are going to be heartbroken, but we have to do it."

"Why?" John Luke asks, joining the two of you. "I was planning on working there all next week."

"I know, John Luke. That's why I'm here. I need both of you to help."

"How so?" you ask.

"During last week's camp we had multiple complaints— three to be exact—of something bothering the campers. All three very different kids, so it's not some prank they're doing for fun." Isaiah looks serious, as if one of his four children were involved in an accident.

3

"Complaints," you repeat. "What sort of complaints?"

"All of them said they saw some kind of ghost."

You have to let out a laugh. "Oh, you know the fun we have with the kids."

"Yeah, I know," Isaiah says. "I know the tales well—have told a few myself. But these stories . . . something's going on. We've alerted the police. There's not a lot we can tell them, though. Nobody's been hurt or attacked. But the kids leaving camp yesterday and today were pretty freaked out."

"What happened?" John Luke asks.

"Two of the kids—a boy and a girl—saw something at night. And another boy reported an 'encounter' in the middle of the woods."

"You kids with your love of being spooked," you say to John Luke. "Someone's always spying in the woods."

Isaiah doesn't smile. "Our fear is that someone might actually be spying. You know. In a not-so-good way."

"Exactly what sort of encounters are you talking about?" you ask.

"The girl saw something—a spirit or a ghost, she thinks—sitting at the end of her bed. In another cabin, a boy said a figure was standing inside, by the window. And the kid in the woods was chased by some kind of beast that jumped down from a tree."

You'd usually be smiling by now, but you notice

4

Isaiah's still not grinning at all. So you just nod. A slight breeze stirs the grass, making the hot and humid weather slightly more bearable. You clean your teeth with a toothpick while you study Isaiah.

John Luke looks serious. "Ghost stories are supposed to be fun. They're not supposed to become real."

"So what would you like us to do?" you ask.

"I'd love John Luke's help—yours too, if that's okay."

"My schedule is pretty busy this week," you say, trying not to laugh, "but I think I might be able to find a little free time."

Isaiah nods. "I know this is a strange request, but I just . . . I was wondering if you guys could spend a night there. I have to leave tomorrow morning for a funeral down in New Orleans and will be gone until Wednesday. Two of my counselors have already left. And, John Luke, you were going to be my third."

"I can do it," John Luke says. "I was gonna be coming out tomorrow morning anyway."

"Yes, but . . ." Isaiah pauses for a moment. "I was hoping for tonight so I could go home and pack for my trip."

"And what do you need?" you ask. "Some Ghostbusters? Want us to bring our guns?"

Isaiah shakes his head. "Something's going on. I just don't know what."

"Then John Luke and I will check it out." You're always ready to help out old friends, even when their requests don't make a whole lot of sense. But this favor comes with a bonus—some one-on-one time with John Luke, which you haven't had in a while.

The camp director sighs with relief. "That's great. It'd be best if you could go over there tonight, but, well, if you want to stay home until the morning, that's fine."

He waits for your reply. You can tell John Luke is ready to leave as soon as possible.

Do you hop in the car and go to
Camp Ch-Yo-Ca right now? Go to page 87.

Do you head to Camp Ch-Yo-Ca tomorrow morning
so you can sleep in your own bed? Go to page 141.

THE CABINS

IT SEEMS LIKE A GOOD TIME to take your stuff to one of the cabins.

The question now is which one you should stay in.

"What do you say, John Luke? We have our pick, don't we?"

"Yeah."

You gaze at the five different cabins where the boys normally sleep. You'll check the girls' cabins in the morning.

"That's the cabin Isaiah said the kid saw something in." John Luke gestures toward it. "We could sleep in there."

"Where do the adults stay?"

"The director's cabin." He points to a sixth cabin that looks the same as the others. It appears to be empty.

"Is that one any nicer?"

"Yeah, a little. And sometimes the crew stacks extra mattresses in there to make the beds softer."

"Let's stay in there!"

"But we didn't hear anything about ghosts showing up in that cabin."

You doubt you'll see a ghost regardless of which cabin you pick, or even if you stay outside under the stars.

Hey, there's a thought. "We could spend the night outdoors. I brought bug spray."

John Luke smiles. "Could be fun."

"It's a nice evening. We could talk for a while. Get some rest. Wake up new men." For you, this is more about bonding with John Luke than finding ghosts anyway. "So what do you say?"

Do you spend the night in the cabin where a ghost was spotted? Go to page 95.

Do you choose the director's cabin? Go to page 185.

Do you sleep outside? Go to page 67.

DUCK DUCK BOO

YOU OPEN THE DOOR but don't see anything. But that's impossible because something was knocking just a sec—

Wait a minute.

You look down and instantly know what's been making this racket at the entrance to the cabin.

It's a duck, and it's staring up at you.

"Go on, get!" You try to shoo it away with your foot.

But the mallard just stays there, gazing at you.

It studies you like you've done something wrong.

"Come on, get out of here." You bend over, trying to wave it into the wilderness.

This mallard, however, doesn't want to budge. Instead it bites your hand. Actually, it doesn't bite but rather snaps at you with its beak. It's not the first time this has happened, and it doesn't really hurt.

Then the duck does it again, and this time you feel something sharp against your skin.

"Ow! Get out of here."

You think about kicking it, but due to the publishing regulations established in 1475, no animal may be unjustly harmed or booted out into the darkness for the sake of great literature or even somewhat-amusing fiction. So you simply guide it away from the doorway with your foot.

You close the door and go back to bed.

About half an hour later, the tapping starts up again. And just like last time, you have barely fallen asleep, so this really annoys you.

You return to the door and find the duck there again. Regarding you with an unflinching gaze. You've never seen a mallard stand still for so long and look at you like that.

You stretch and glance around. *Am I dreaming?*

But the balmy night air. The noises of the forest. The sound of John Luke turning on his mattress. You're awake. Wide-awake.

You reach down and pick up the duck, cradling it in your arms so it won't move. Then you head to the woods behind your cabin and set the duck on the grass.

"Okay, go on, buddy. Go find your brace of ducks. I'm sure they're somewhere around here."

The mallard just stands there, still staring at you, not moving. Something's clearly wrong with it. But you're not gonna check it over nor bring it to the vet. What kind of Duck Commander would bring a duck to the vet?

You hope you can end this little story nugget right here. You walk away and assume you'll never see the duck again.

Oh, but that would be too normal, wouldn't it?

Goodness knows you only want to sleep. It's around one in the morning when you return to bed.

Sleep almost finds you. You're so close. But then . . .

Tap-tap-tap.

Not again.

Tap-tap-tap.

This is almost enough to make you curse, but you're not a cursing man. You gave that up when you turned your life over to God. But this duck sure is trying to provoke your tired soul.

You sit up and shake your head.

It's time.

The duck had its chance. Twice now.

You open the door and come face-to-face with the mallard. But then you see another and another and

There have to be about a hundred of them, all standing in front of your cabin. All facing you. All glaring at you.

Hundreds of ducks looking you straight in the eye as if you've done something wrong.

Hundreds of angry ducks.

Do you wake John Luke and get out of here? Go to page 135.

Do you deal with the ducks right here and now (even though it's not duck-hunting season)? Go to page 31.

HUNGRY

EVEN THOUGH MISS KAY ENCOURAGES YOU to head to the hospital with John Luke, you decide to stay home until morning. You don't need to be rushing to the ER in the middle of the night. There's no reason. You got some deep bites from an animal, sure. But you've had worse. Miss Kay helped you clean it up and get it bandaged, and you feel normal now. Just a bit warm.

"I don't want your arm to get infected," Miss Kay says.

"Oh, I'm fine. I don't want to wake up John Luke."

You convince her to head back to bed, and you take a seat in your recliner. "I'm gonna read for a while and see if I get tired." It's a little after two, but you're still wide-awake. *This is the problem with being woken up in the middle of the night.*

You pick up a history book that you're halfway through. As you do, you can feel yourself shivering.

That's weird. It's not that cold in here.

You focus on the text, and suddenly you can see the individual dots of ink that make up each letter. Your heart begins to slow, and now you're feeling tired. So tired that it's hard to keep your eyes open.

Also, you have this weird craving for meat. Like a big, juicy steak. A rib eye. A New York strip.

Or maybe a plump pork chop. Or how about some ribs?

Your mouth is watering.

And you have no idea why because you had a big Sunday night dinner.

You blink, and everything turns red. The pain in your arm is throbbing, and you feel like you might explode.

It might be time to go to the hospital. But when you stand, you notice something really strange.

No, it's beyond strange. It's cuckoo land.

Your bare feet are . . . not feet anymore.

They're paws. Wolf paws.

You're changing before your very eyes. Your hands, your arms.

The full moon . . . the howling in the trees . . . the big creature biting you . . .

You know now what all this means.

So werewolves *do* exist. If only you could tell the boys. You bet they'd love to go hunting after them.

Maybe in a short time they'll be hunting after you.

14

You let out a roaring cry and know the end is near.

In fact . . . it might already be here.

Am I a wolf yet? You stumble into the bathroom to examine the situation. Yep, fur covers your arms and legs . . . and feet. Your feet—uh, paws—are really furry, in fact. But that's it. *Man, I always thought turning into a werewolf would be a lot more interesting than getting hobbit feet.*

THE END?

A QUILL OF JOHN LUKE

YOU STAY ONSHORE as John Luke rolls up his pant legs and wades into the lake after the floating feathers. It takes him a while to retrieve them, but he manages to avoid getting completely wet. Soon he's holding all four in his hands.

As he steps onto the beach, the strangest thing happens.

You get a whiff of something really bad. Like *death* bad.

"John Luke, you smell that?"

"Yeah. I think it's these." He holds the feathers as far from his body as possible.

You go over and smell the feathers in his hand. They reek worse than anything you've ever experienced.

"What's wrong with those things?"

John Luke jerks his head back even farther from the feathers. "Ugh. The feather we found in the gym didn't smell."

"Chief Stinkum." You raise your eyebrows.

He laughs but examines the feathers suspiciously.

You don't find any other feathers in the area, so you head back to the cabins. For some reason John Luke keeps sniffing the plumes in his hand, then holding them far away again.

"Do you like that smell?" you finally ask.

"Only three of them stink."

"Okay. Throw them away."

"But don't you see, Papaw Phil? Three of them stink. One doesn't."

You stop as John Luke holds the feathers up, three in one hand and one in the other.

"It's the legend! Of Chief Stinkum's four sons. These three smell horrible, but this one doesn't."

"So did someone at camp spread stink sauce all over those three? To have some fun with us?"

John Luke shakes his head and peers into the trees and bushes as if someone might jump out. Perhaps the Lone Ranger and Tonto. Or maybe General Custer, preparing for his last stand.

Or maybe a guy ready to put the two of us in white straitjackets.

"Well, you keep those sealed up tight, John Luke. Something to remind you of the camp. Or a really bad outhouse."

You turn to John Luke when he doesn't reply. He seems to be in some kind of trance.

"You okay, John Luke?"

He nods but doesn't say a word.

• • •

Later that night, after falling asleep in a bottom bunk across from John Luke's bed, you're awakened by a strange sound.

Someone's yelling outside the cabin.

You sit up and call into the darkness, "John Luke, you hear that?"

He doesn't respond.

The voice outside keeps wailing. "Heyyyaaaa heeeyyyy-yyyaaaa *heeeeyyyyyyaaaahhhh.*"

It sounds like someone trying to do a chant. Except they're really bad at it.

Like those pale imitation duck calls compared to Duck Commander calls.

You pat the bed across from yours, expecting to find John Luke and shake him. But the bed is empty. The blanket is pulled back.

"John Luke?" you call again.

The *heyyyaaahh* sound outside continues.

You stumble around until you locate the light switch. But John Luke is nowhere to be found.

The chant changes wording a little but remains loud as ever. "Oh-way oh-way way-oh!"

This is crazy. Someone's outside your door pretending to be a warrior or rain dancer or something. Except he sounds a lot like Kermit the Frog.

You open the door expecting to find someone you know playing a prank. Maybe one of your sons. Instead you see a fire burning in the middle of the camp with someone else dancing around it.

That's not someone else—that's John Luke! Is it really him?

He's wearing only jeans with his face and chest painted red. The four feathers are stuck in his hair.

"Staaaankkkkk-oohhhhhh wannkkkkk-oooooohhhh."

He's got something in his hand, something resembling a spear. But when you get closer to him, you see it's only a long stick.

"John Luke, what are you doing?"

But he doesn't hear you. He's in another world. He stops dancing around the fire and holds the stick over his head.

"Waaaaackkkemmmmm wackkkkkeeemmmmm wooo-eeeeeeee."

You approach to take the stick away from him, but he catches sight of you and his eyes widen. Then he jumps across the fire—*through* the flames—and runs full speed into the woods.

"Aaaaaaeeeeee aaaaaaeeeee aaaaaaaaahh!" he screams as he heads into the darkness. "Saaaackkkkkaaaaa blacckaaaaa bbb—"

He's cut off by a loud and sudden thud.

The chanting is no more.

"John Luke?"

You rush into the woods and find him about fifty yards in. Looks like he ran into a tree and knocked himself out.

You pick Chief John Lukem up and carry him back to the cabin. As you pass the fire, you pull the feathers out of his hair and throw them into the flames. They burn quickly.

John Luke's eyes open while he's still in your arms.

"Chief Stinkum?" he asks in mumbled words.

"That's me. And I'm gonna make you smell real nice. You just take it easy."

You've seen enough of this camp for one night. You decide to take John Luke to the hospital to get his head checked for a concussion.

You'll also ask if they can maybe give him a shower. Cause woo-hooo. The boy really stinks.

THE END

CHASE

JOHN LUKE STAYS BEHIND to keep watch while you sprint toward the woods, where the noise seems to have come from. Well, you don't really sprint—more like a fast jog. You're not as lightning fast as you used to be, but you can still run. You feel pretty good about yourself at sixty-eight years old in your boots, camo pants, and T-shirt.

Just don't trip since you're running with a machete.

You'd probably tell most people not to run through the woods with a long knife.

Then again, you've seen some crazy things in woods like these over the years.

You once met a guy in the backwoods who wore only underwear and planned to live off the land. You and a buddy named Mac had to talk the guy back home. Oh, and this person also had a gun.

Lots of folks have guns around here.

And I'm just carrying a machete.

You stop after running for a few minutes. You can feel your heart racing.

Then you hear it.

Ch-ch-ch-ka-ka-ka.

It's coming from your right.

You take a dozen steps or so until . . . the ground beneath you disappears.

You fall about six feet and land on your back.

The last thing you see before losing consciousness is the shadow of a large person. He's not carrying a machete, however. He's carrying a long spear.

You try to call out—to say something—but you're too much out of breath. As the man comes closer, you realize he's wearing some kind of mask.

He raises the spear.

And your vision fades.

• • •

When you wake up, a couple men are helping you out of the pit.

Where'd they come from?

When you reach the top of the hole, you notice flashing lights everywhere. The men place you on a stretcher, but you tell them you're fine. "Where's John Luke?"

Then you spot him standing next to the closest ambulance. You're told he's the one who called the police after running off a crazy person with a spear.

You want to scold him for following you into the woods, but there's a more pressing question on your mind. "How'd you scare him off?"

"He had a spear, but I had a rifle. When he saw it, he ran away."

You finally agree to go to the hospital, but besides a few broken ribs, everything is fine.

You never find out who the guy with the spear was. He doesn't come around again. But everybody assumes it was the same person who was messing around the camp. The authorities discover several more pits near the camp, exactly the same as the one you fell into. They were intended to be traps for animals, it seems.

You keep the machete, and life at Camp Ch-Yo-Ca goes back to normal again. No more reports of ghosts or spooky noises.

But every now and then, on a quiet evening, you can still hear the chanting.

Ch-ch-ch-ka-ka-ka.

Maybe it's just something haunting your dreams.

Maybe the animals around your property would know.

THE END

FLUFFBALLS

"LET'S CLEAN SOME OF THIS STUFF UP," you tell John Luke. "Maybe the spiders will leave if we do."

"Should we call anybody?"

"Let's just work for a while and see how it goes. We'll think about who can help us out later."

You won't contact any authorities unless you have to—someone might end up talking to the press about this. You don't want the camp to get a bad name, and ten thousand yards of spiderwebs covering the grounds sure won't help.

You ask John Luke where some shovels might be, and he leads you to a maintenance shed. You both peel off the thick layer of cobwebs coating the building and grab a shovel apiece.

"We're going to make a big fire with all these webs," you say, making your way to the first cobweb-covered cabin. "Maybe we'll burn some of the spiders while we're at it."

But this sounds simpler than it is. The webs simply want to stick to the end of the shovel, no matter how hard you shake it. So after scooping up a big wad of them resembling a massive stick of cotton candy, you use the bottom of your boot to scrape off the stuff. After about an hour of this, you guys have made a nice gooey pile of white.

You get some gasoline and light the webs on fire.

The cobwebs burn slowly and reluctantly. It takes more gas to keep the fire going. You decide to put some wood on it to make sure the flames last.

All that work, and you've only managed to clear one cabin so far.

The fire begins to die down again, in spite of the wood. "John Luke, go see if you can find some newspaper. Maybe check the director's cabin."

He disappears for a minute.

Then you hear a loud scream.

When you look toward the director's cabin, there's no sign of John Luke. At first. Until you spot the flailing arms and legs on the ground.

It's him.

And he's got a massive black, hairy spider . . . *on his face*.

Do you run over and yank the creature off of John Luke? Go to page 91.

Do you grab some gloves and a knife before helping him? Go to page 103.

QUACK QUACK

SHOOTING AT THOSE DUCKS WASN'T THE BEST PLAN.
Willie has to come pay your bail and get you out of jail.

"Disturbing the peace?" he asks, shaking his head.

"Did you see all those ducks?"

"I didn't see a single one," Willie says. "John Luke thinks you've lost your mind. What were you doing firing a gun in the middle of the night at the camp? You almost shot the policeman who was approaching you."

"I was attacked by ducks! I went to get my gun, and once I had it, they all started coming after me."

"Uh-huh. You feeling okay? I mean, did you eat anything crazy tonight?"

"I know what I saw," you insist. "I grabbed my gun and they attacked. It was like *Gladiator* out there. I was surrounded and had to fight them off on all sides."

"*Gladiator*?" Willie shakes his head. "I'm telling Mom that you need some rest."

"You didn't find any ducks? Not one?"

"Nope."

"Then there's some conspiracy going on because I know what I shot. I got a dozen of them. At least."

"It's off-season. You can't go around *shooting* ducks, even if they are there. And there's no way you could hit that many."

"You sure can when they're attacking you!" This was clearly self-defense.

Willie stares at you for a very long time.

"They were giving me looks *just* like that," you mutter.

"You need some sleep."

You follow him out to his truck and get inside. "Something's going on at the camp, Willie."

"Not anymore," he says. "Target practice is over. Next time you'll have to spend the night in jail."

As he pulls away from the sheriff's building, you spot them in the grass on the corner.

A group of mallards, all standing still and staring at you.

Watching you as Willie takes you home.

You don't say a thing about them. Maybe Willie's right. Maybe you're super tired and just need some sleep. But then again . . .

THE END

THE STRANGER

"LET'S PICK HIM UP," you tell John Luke, and he comes to a stop. "He looks pretty harmless."

Some of the weirdest men and women who have ever lived and breathed on this earth have appeared the most normal. So having long hair and a beard doesn't mean anything. In fact, to you, it seems sorta right. Unless the beard happens to be on a woman, in which case you might have to immediately run and get out of there.

The guy doesn't rush to your car but walks slowly. "Appreciate you stoppin'," he says with a thick Louisiana accent that's got a bit of Cajun in it.

"How you doin'?" you ask the guy as he enters the backseat.

"Good, good. I'm just headin' over to Cal . . ."

You swear he said California. "What was that?"

"Calhoun."

"Well, we can take you part of the way."

John Luke smiles and wrinkles his nose. You know he's surely smelling what you're smelling. Some really bad body odor. Major capital boldfaced **BO!** with an exclamation point after it.

Maybe the man is homeless and hasn't had the opportunity to take a bath in a while.

"You live in Calhoun?" you ask.

"Just passin' through. Originally from New Orleans."

"Some fine cookin' down in those parts."

He mumbles something you don't quite understand. Then he speaks up in a more intelligible tone. "You're those Robertsons, right? The duck family?"

"That be us. This is John Luke, my chauffeur and grandson."

"My name's Otis. Visited you guys' store the other day. You got a big operation."

"God has been very good to us."

"Nice to hear he's good to *someone*. 'Cause it sure seems like he loves ignorin' some folks."

You turn to look at Otis. "Do you know your heavenly Father?"

"Every now and then."

It's an interesting comment. *"Every now and then."*

"So you pass him by every now and then?" you ask. "Like a hitchhiker on the road?"

"I got some family issues. They get on me and I get on them."

"Well, those issues aren't too big for God," you simply say. "God loves you, you know that?"

He doesn't reply, so you don't push.

After a minute of silence, Otis asks, "You guys really hunters, or is that all for show?"

You turn again. "Think this beard's for show?"

"Reckon not."

"It's real," you say. "It's all real. Hunting and fishing's been a big part of my life. Always."

"Yeah. That's cool."

"Yes, it is."

You reach the entrance to the camp, and John Luke slows down.

"Well, this is as far as we're going," you inform your passenger.

"What's this place?"

"A Christian camp," John Luke says.

Otis opens the door. "I 'member going to camp when I was a kid. Got lost in the woods and had to spend the night out there. Scared the daylights out of me." He shakes his head. "Well, thanks for the ride. Y'all have a good one."

"You too."

"Don't let anything kidnap you in those woods

tonight." Otis lets out a menacing sort of laugh as he continues down the road.

As you drive into the camp and pass the sign, you can smell Otis even though he's not in the Jeep anymore.

John Luke takes a gradual curve. "Wonder what he's doing around here?"

"Just passin' through, he said. Lots of folks live their life just passin' through."

The road winds through thick woods, and soon you're near the soccer field. The camp buildings are just up ahead, all tucked around each other. It's unusual not to see a hundred kids around here, especially at this time of year.

"So does it look haunted to you, John Luke?"

He shrugs. "Maybe the ghost of Zodie Sims is hanging out here."

"You're gonna have to tell me about that one later."

He parks the Jeep and you both get out.

"Well, think we can make it a whole night here by ourselves?" you ask John Luke.

"Surely someone's still here. Want to go see?"

Do you try to find someone? Go to page 99.

Do you drop off your stuff in one of the cabins? Go to page 7.

THE PLAN

IT TAKES YOU ABOUT TWENTY MINUTES to move all the mattresses back to their bunk beds. They're heavier than you thought they'd be. "Whoever did this went to a lot of trouble."

"Someone's messin' with us," John Luke mutters.

"You think so?"

"Yeah—they might've overheard us talking."

You head into the bathroom, where you placed your shaving kit earlier, and spot something strange right away. A message is written across all five mirrors above the sinks.

The message is written in toothpaste. *Your* toothpaste.

It reads, *You don't know the truth.*

"John Luke!"

He enters and reads the message.

"Did you see or hear anybody come in here?" you ask.

"No, sir."

"I just placed my bag on the sink an hour ago."

"That's really weird."

You nod. "It's really wasteful is what it is. That's some good toothpaste—it's the whitening kind."

"Still don't believe in ghosts?" John Luke sounds kinda worried.

You stare at the words on the mirrors. "I can't believe someone's trying to make life miserable for people at this camp. And now that includes us."

"You think someone did this to scare us?"

"That's what I think."

"So what should we do?"

You take your toothbrush and help yourself to the paste from one of the letters on the mirror.

"We stay here and see what happens," you say. "I have an idea too."

"What?"

You shake your head, knowing someone could be listening. "Just an idea. That's all. Brush your teeth. You can use some of my toothpaste. Then it's time for bed."

About fifteen minutes later you can hear John Luke's steady breathing, signaling he's asleep. You slip out of bed without any noise. You've only had sixty-eight years to master the art of being quiet, after all. You don't turn on a light, nor do you open the front door—the back door through the bathroom will be the perfect exit.

The white toothpaste on the mirror glows as you pass by. *I'll get it off tomorrow.*

Or maybe tonight you'll make someone else get it off, if everything goes according to plan.

The door to the outside creaks slightly, but not too much. You slide out and shut it behind you.

The question is where to go keep watch.

You end up picking a large tree about twenty yards from the cabin. Here, you'll be able to see both the front of the building and the doorway from the bathroom. Propping your back up against the tree, you settle in to keep an eye on things.

Do you fall asleep? Go to page 217.

Do you stay awake? Go to page 225.

WHO LET THE DOGS OUT?

WHOEVER IS HAVING FUN making noises in the woods will just have to wait. It's bedtime for you. You turn on the bathroom light again and finish brushing your teeth. It's pretty humid and sticky in here—hopefully there are some fans around to cool it down.

You head out to your bunk bed and straighten your sleeping bag as John Luke takes his toothbrush into the bathroom.

In about thirty seconds you hear his loud moan.

"Uh, Papaw Phil," he shouts. "I think I found another animal."

You go in there and join John Luke in front of the middle stall.

"It's *in* the toilet," he says.

Well, that's rather unfortunate.

"Get it out then," you tell him. "Throw it away."

"This is nasty," he says.

But he does it. This time, however, he finds some gloves in the storage closet first.

You search the rest of the cabin for other funky surprises but don't find anything.

You lie down on your bed, but after the events of the night, you're more wound up than you thought. Normally you'd be able to sit in your La-Z-Boy and watch some action movie on television until you get tired. But tonight, it's just you and John Luke.

"Let's build a fire," you suggest.

There's a fire pit right outside, at the center of the boys' cabins, and you both gather wood and pile it up. Soon the fire is blazing, and the two of you are sitting next to it, watching it crackle and wave.

"You think someone's really doing all this stuff to frighten the kids around here?" John Luke asks.

For some reason you think of a story from years ago that you decide John Luke is old enough to hear.

"Did anybody ever tell you about the dog thief they had around these parts years ago?"

John Luke looks at you to see if you're joking. "A dog that was a thief?"

"No, no—a guy who stole dogs. It had to be—let's see— oh, this was before Willie and Korie moved here to help with the camp. I think it was during the nineties."

"Someone was kidnapping dogs?"

"Yeah. Dozens of them. At first the police just thought it was some weird coincidence. Dogs running away here and there. But then they realized some nut job was going around taking them. You know how easy it'd be? He tricked them by feeding them treats. Dogs are dumb—they'll eat anything."

"Wow. Did he get arrested?"

You nod. "Yeah. Someone reported him for suspicious behavior, and he confessed. He was proud of it. So he served some time. Got out. But then he got into some other trouble. Sin catches up to you."

The scent of the fire distracts you, making you hungry again. You wish you'd brought something to make s'mores with.

"You don't think there's another person around like that guy?"

"I don't think so," you say. "But if there is, he'll get found."

You notice John Luke doesn't look too sure about sitting outside surrounded by dark woods.

"Don't you worry about us," you reassure him. "We can trust in God's protection. And I have the machete in case anybody wakes me up."

John Luke laughs, knowing it's best *not* to wake you up.

In addition to the crickets chirping and the fire crackling, you suddenly hear something else.

A high-pitched scream.

You look at John Luke.

That didn't sound good.

It's one thing to hear strange noises coming from the woods. Or to find a dead animal. But to hear a scream like that—as if someone's in trouble or hurting—is entirely another thing.

You need to see what's happening. But you also need to be careful with your grandson.

Do you tell John Luke to go inside the cabin and then check out the scream yourself? Go to page 127.

Do you check out the scream with John Luke and your machete? Go to page 199.

Do you call the cops and drive home? Go to page 179.

THE BABY OF
THE FAMILY

YOU FEEL BETTER with your rifle in hand. It's always been like this. Out in the woods, it's natural to walk around with a gun. A predator searching for his kill. At the grocery store or the pharmacy, however, they don't like it much when you're toting around your gun. Which is sad 'cause you certainly would like to take it with you wherever you go. The donut shop. The cleaners. An amusement park.

You head toward the gnawing sounds. They keep getting louder and louder.

The trees and the darkness are your friends right now. You blend in like a panther. Or a phantom.

You hear a different sound—more of a crackling—and turn to see some kind of strange light. Little flickers dance off the trees. *It's a fire.*

You see a figure standing next to the blaze.

It's the monster. The thing of John Luke's stories. This animal appears to be a creature of the dark pit of night. A hideous beast so foul, you've never seen the likes of it.

An allibeaver.

I'm gonna get you and stuff you and put you over our television.

You grip your gun and raise it toward the figure.

Then you see something else happening.

The beast begins to peel off its skin. Literally.

Okay, I'm not dreaming, so what am I seeing here?

Suddenly you realize this is someone—a man—taking off a costume. He turns and you see a familiar face.

"Dad?" It's Jep, your youngest son.

"Jeptha, what are you doing?"

"Shhh," Jep says, glancing all around.

"You know you almost got shot in that costume of yours."

"We're making a film," he says.

"Who's 'we'?"

"Oh, they're all around. The filmmakers. It's great. We're gonna make a bona fide horror movie."

"Starring who?"

"You," Jep says. "You and John Luke."

"Nope. Don't think so."

"Shhh," he says again, approaching you. When he gets close, he whispers, "They're everywhere."

48

"Good. Then they can hear me."

"Just go with the program. This is going to be great."

"'This'? What do you mean by 'this'?"

"A Halloween special. It's called *Die, Duck Commander, Die*."

You give Jep a look.

"I don't think so," you tell him. "It's late and I need some sleep."

You start to head back to your sleeping bag and John Luke. Jep calls out for you in the darkness. "Dad?"

But you keep walking.

"Will you just be in this one allibeaver scene? Please?"

You shake your head. Is it possible Jep and his little movie were seriously the cause of all the fears and worries around the camp? Unbelievable. And the movie doesn't even look like it'll be very good.

Youth really is wasted on the young.

THE END

VIBES

YOU STARE ACROSS THE LAKE. It's not big—you could probably swim to the other side without any problem. The water is still, the moon hovering over the tops of the trees. John Luke is texting someone.

"There you go again. Always sending your texts. *Boo bee boo bee boo.*" You act like you're holding a phone and tapping on it. He's used to this from you. "You know what's great about not having a cell phone?"

He doesn't look up. "What?"

"You get to enjoy all this." You point to the lake and the trees beyond it.

All of a sudden you hear a noise.

"What was that?" you ask.

"What?"

"Did you hear something?"

John Luke shakes his head.

You stand at the edge of the lake and squint. Only silence. And then . . .

Ch-ch-ch-ka-ka-ka.

"There—that sound. Didn't you hear it?"

"No."

"Are you making noises on your phone?"

"No, sir," John Luke says, slipping the phone back into his jeans pocket.

You peer into the forest, trying to see if someone's out there. But you can't spot anything out of the ordinary.

"Let's go back to the cabins," you say. "It's gonna be dark before we know it."

As you start to retrace your steps, you hear another *ch-ch-ch*. You stop cold.

The sound stops with you.

When you resume walking, it begins again.

Ka-ka-ka.

"You didn't hear that, John Luke?"

"No."

"Then I think my hearin's going, or I'm imagining things."

"Maybe it's the ghost."

"Maybe."

"Hi, ghost!" John Luke shouts.

The sound goes off again.

Ch-ch-ch-ka-ka-ka.

When you get to the edge of the woods, you notice something sticking out of a tree. You walk over and try to pull it out. Looks like some kind of knife. "You ever seen this before, John Luke?"

"No. We would never have a knife like that where the kids could find it. What should we do with it?"

**Do you continue trying to pull
the blade out of the tree?
Go to page 75.**

**Do you leave the weapon here and head
to the cabins? It's kind of late and dark to
be examining this kind of evidence.
Go to page 7.**

SCREAMING
FOR BUBBLES

"GET OUT OF THERE!" you yell at John Luke as his head emerges.

Just as he turns in the water, the massive spider is on him. You still can't believe how fast the creature is moving. Now the spider is clamped onto John Luke, and it drags him under the water.

Did that just happen?

"No!"

The surface of the water gets very still.

"No!" you scream again.

Then you notice slight bubbles emerging from the lake. You stop screaming and the bubbles go away. You start screaming again and they continue.

"No!" equals bubbles.

Silence equals no bubbles.

Soon you see something bobbing up and down in the water.

It's John Luke. He sucks in air and starts swimming back to land.

"What happened?" you ask, confused but relieved.

But he seems too out of breath to answer.

As he starts to get out of the water, Si appears from the top of the hill. He's holding a shotgun. John Luke is dripping and gasping.

"You guys okay?" Si asks.

"Are *you* okay, John Luke?"

He nods and looks back at the water.

"Why are you all wet?" Si asks.

"I was hot."

Si shakes his head. "What's with all these cobwebs everywhere? You guys seen any big spiders around?"

"I just punched one in the face underwater," John Luke says. He flexes his arms like a prizefighter.

You throw him his shirt. "Dry off, Rocky."

"This place needs to be quarantined, Jack," Si says.

You don't see anything else in the water, and you're sure glad whatever it was that attacked John Luke hasn't reemerged.

"John Luke, I think it's time we got out of here."

"Hey, Jack. What about me?"

You turn to Si and pat him on the back. "You hold down the fort. We'll send you some reinforcements."

"Who's that?"

"Oh, we'll get Willie and Jase and Jep to come over here. That'll be enough. You think, John Luke?"

He nods at Si as you both start walking up the hill, leaving Si to continue talking.

"Hey, man, this is serious stuff here! You see these cobwebs? They gotta belong to some ten-foot-tall spider. I mean, I once saw one over in 'Nam, and it had to be about fifteen feet tall, and I'm telling you, I got . . ."

THE END

SCENE OF THE CRIME

JOHN LUKE GIVES YOU A BIG HUG when you get inside the Jeep.

"There was a dude with a gas can who lit the whole place on fire," he says, talking so fast he loses his breath.

"And where'd he go?" you ask, looking around to make sure you're not going to be attacked.

"Into the woods. I called the cops, and I called Dad too. They're on their way."

"Move over. I'll drive," you tell him.

The strange noises and mysterious happenings were concerning, but this threat is real and it's dangerous.

You start up the Jeep and make your way back to the main road.

"Call your mother and tell her you're okay."

"She probably knows. I told Dad—"

"If she doesn't, then you'll be the first to tell her. It's better she knows you're okay than to give her a scare."

You're passing the soccer field when you jam on the brake. The Jeep skids to a stop, and both of you are caught by your seat belts.

In front of you is a tall figure wearing camo, his face painted black. He's got a backpack over his shoulder that's bulging with stuff. He stands for a moment before raising a hand toward his face.

"John Luke, get down," you shout as you do the same.

Then you hear something. Something familiar.

A duck call.

The guy in front of you is blowing a duck call.

That's a Duck Commander Mallard Drake call.

The man bolts across the soccer field and into the woods beyond. He's going too fast for you to chase him.

You're about to call the cops again when you see the flashing lights of police cars and fire engines racing toward you.

Do you wait for the police to come over when
they need you? Turn to page 235.

Do you talk to the police right away?
You want answers! Turn to page 139.

LOUISIANA CHAINSAW MASSACRE

SURE, YOU HEARD what sounded like a tree falling down in the middle of the night. But that tree will still be there in the morning, and the woods will be a lot less creepy then. You decide to go back to sleep and tell John Luke to do the same.

Better to simply be safe.

Better to simply be careful.

Of course, great men and women in history haven't become great by playing it simple and safe and careful, have they?

This time, a part of you simply says, "Oh, well."

But "Oh, well" isn't gonna cut it (no pun intended) when you're awakened again by the sound of a chainsaw.

A chainsaw that happens to be *right outside your cabin door*.

You jerk up and hit your head on the frame of the bunk above you. The chainsaw is roaring, and you realize that it's not just outside your cabin door.

It's cutting into the door.

Doing the simple and safe thing suddenly makes you feel really stupid.

"John Luke, get up!"

Not that you actually have to tell him. He's already jumping around the cabin and generally freaking out.

You think about informing him that there's a chainsaw chewing through the cabin door, but you assume he sorta knows this.

You grab him by the shoulders. "Is there a back door to this place?" you shout.

"Yeah," he yells above the *weeeeerrrrrrweeeerrrrr*.

"Where is it?"

"It's the door! In the back."

That's absolutely not helpful.

"You go and I'll follow," you tell him.

The chainsaw is destroying the door. Whoever's doing this might as well kick the door in at this point. But the chainsaw just keeps grinding away.

John Luke takes you into the bathroom and through another door leading out of the cabin. You both run full speed for the shelter of the trees. The chainsaw is still running, but it soon sounds distant. Your escape isn't complete yet, though.

"Where should we go?" John Luke asks under his breath.

"Where are your car keys?"

"In my jeans," he says.

You look down and see he's wearing his pajama shorts.

"What about your cell phone?"

"In my jeans."

You sigh and nod. You might normally ask him where he keeps his brain, but now's not the time to be funny. You can be funny when people are opening presents or eating cake or sipping coffee or watching TV, but it's definitely not a good time when someone's grinding down your door with a chainsaw.

"Is your Jeep open?" you ask.

"Yeah."

"You still have your rifle in the back?"

"Yeah."

"Okay. Let's circle around through the trees to make sure we're far away from the cabin. Then I'll make a break for the car."

"Who is this person?"

"I don't know, but whoever it is, is gonna pay. I don't like being woken up."

You and John Luke scramble through the woods and sneak in the direction of the Jeep. The chainsaw sound has stopped for the moment. But that could be worse, because now you imagine someone creeping around with a massive weapon in his hands.

Maybe it's just a local guy from the forest preserve doing some testing.

Yes, and maybe it's Elvis visiting the camp and carrying a chainsaw instead of a guitar.

"Love me tender, love me—weeeeerrrrrrrrweeeeerrrrrr."

You both manage to make it over to the part of the woods closest to John Luke's Jeep. The vehicle's silhouette can be seen from your spot behind the trees.

But it's still way too quiet for your liking.

**Do you make your way to the Jeep to get the rifle?
Go to page 161.**

**Do you stay behind the trees with John Luke until
you know the stranger is gone? Go to page 121.**

A TALE TOO TERRIFYING FOR THE KIDS

"YEAH, LET'S SLEEP OUTSIDE," John Luke says. "If anything sketchy is going on, we'll hear it from out here."

"Right. Let's make a big fire and put lots of bug spray on and tell some spooky stories. See who—or *what*—comes to visit us." You raise your eyebrows, and John Luke rolls his eyes.

He knows the perfect spot for your sleeping bags. You guys don't have a tent, but that's okay. You'll be able to spot the monsters or aliens or bogeymen better this way.

After a few minutes, you have a good fire going and suddenly wish you'd brought some stuff to make s'mores with. It's not that you're hungry, but you've got to have a little something to eat when you're around a fire, right? Especially at camp.

You lean forward on the log that serves as a bench. "So let's hear one of those ghost stories you kids tell."

"Which one?"

"Any of them. The scarier the better." You toss a piece of wood onto the fire while John Luke thinks.

"Well, the one I always tell is about the allibeaver."

You nod like you know what that is. "An allibeaver. Oh, this is gonna be good."

"Years ago, one of the directors here had a pet beaver. All the kids loved him. He was a friendly little guy who made everybody laugh. But one night he escaped from his cage."

"Uh-oh."

"He wandered down to the lake, and this big alligator bit him. But it wasn't no ordinary gator. This one was infected with some awful disease. Once he bit the beaver, it turned into an allibeaver."

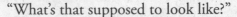

"What's that supposed to look like?"

John Luke laughs. "It's got the face of an alligator and the body of a beaver. So it can climb things but also tear off someone's head with its long gator mouth."

"I'd love to see one of those."

John Luke is about to keep talking when you both hear something fall in the woods with a loud, heavy thud.

"What was that?" you ask.

"I don't know."

Maybe it's an allibeaver responding to the sound of its name.
You probably won't share that thought with John Luke.

"Keep talking," you tell him.

"Now the allibeaver sneaks into the cabins and starts infecting the kids. When they're bitten, though, they don't die. They become allibeavers too. And they can walk around and infect other people."

"Do they have tails?"

"Uh, yeah. And sharp teeth like gators."

"This is the most terrifyin' thing I've ever heard." You smirk.

"There's only one way to stop an allibeaver."

"What's that?"

"You have to kill it, and then everyone it's bitten turns back into themselves. But you can't just shoot the allibeaver. You have to cut off its tail."

"Wow, that's too much for me." You shake your head and drop another piece of wood onto the fire. "So who does the choppin' in your story?"

"Sometimes it's me. Sometimes Dad. Sometimes it's nobody, and the allibeaver infects everybody at the camp, who then go home and infect more."

Another thudding sound echoes from the woods.

"Maybe it's the allibeaver," John Luke says, only half-laughing. Great minds think alike.

**Do you and John Luke try to find
what's in the woods?
Go to page 173.**

**Do you stay by the fire and go to sleep?
Go to page 163.**

THE HUNTER

YOU WAIT A FEW MINUTES and hear the wailing sound again. This time it's farther away from you, deeper in the woods. You follow it.

You've hunted animals many times at night, so this is no different.

The trail leads you through the trees and over a hill. It's cooler outside now and the sky above is clear, allowing enough light through the treetops that you don't need to use your flashlight.

The animal scream rings out again. You're getting closer.

You keep your rifle pointed in front of you, not wanting to be caught off guard by some kind of rabid beast. You imagine the headline: *Duck Commander Phil Robertson Attacked by Wild Animal in the Middle of the Night.*

At that moment, you make out another sound, distinct

from the first one. It's a deep, heavy panting sound, almost like a big dog.

Or how about a wolf?

You look at the moon and notice it's full. You didn't realize this earlier.

The howling surrounds you again. This time it definitely sounds like some kind of wolf. Except it's more intense than any wolf you've ever heard.

The bushes in front of you shake with a wild, loud scampering noise.

Then . . .

Something rushes at you from the right. Attacks you. Crashes into you, bites your right forearm, and forces you to drop the rifle.

But you manage to pick up the weapon again and fire at the big, hairy beast. Once. Twice.

Yet it's gone.

The pain in your arm is intense. You touch it with your left hand and can feel the warm blood.

You use the flashlight to survey the land around you. But you don't see or hear anything.

You better go get this wound treated.

ROBERTSON AND THRASHER

Do you go to the hospital just in case you
need a rabies shot? Go to page 153.

Do you bandage the wound at home?
Go to page 13.

STAGED

YOU FINALLY MANAGE TO WIGGLE the blade out of the trunk. It's more than just a knife—you're holding a machete in your hands. "Look at this. It's gotta be about an eighteen- or twenty-inch blade."

As you turn the machete to examine it, you see something you wish you would have noticed sooner. Something red.

Something that looks exactly like blood.

And it appears to be fresh.

• • •

It takes about ten minutes for John Luke to locate where the blood might have come from.

"Hey, Papaw Phil. I think I found something."

John Luke is standing near the outdoor theater with seats in a half circle descending the hill. He points to the stage, where oftentimes a worship leader speaks to the campers and leads music. Lots of songs and prayers have been offered up from this little section of the world right here.

"Do you see that?" he says.

Both of you walk down the hill and step onto the wooden platform.

Sure enough, there's some type of animal in the middle of the stage. And it's not moving, even when you poke it with the machete.

You've seen plenty of dead animals before, and so has John Luke, so the sight doesn't gross you out. But you are a bit fascinated with why this particular one might have been left here. Is it a message?

"Well, can't just leave this thing in the middle of the theater," you say. "Let's clean it up and head back . . . after we've secured the perimeter."

Before leaving, the two of you search the stage for a few minutes but can't find any other clues.

Eventually, you give up and tell John Luke to deposit the animal in a nearby garbage can. "Don't get guts on you," you warn John Luke. "Your mom won't like that."

"*I* won't like that," he replies.

As you climb the hill out of the theater, the machete at your side, John Luke asks, "You think this has anything to do with the stuff that was reported?"

"I think this machete had something to do with that animal," you say. "And I think someone's having a good ole time laughing about it. That's what I think."

You head toward the cabins to unload your gear and settle in for the night, and as you walk, you notice how thick the woods around you are. You scan them intently, looking for anything or anybody. But nobody's out there—not within your line of sight, at least.

At the cabin, John Luke goes straight to the bathroom to wash his hands.

"We'll look things over again tomorrow," you call from your seat on a bottom bunk.

That's the moment you hear the sound again.

Ch-ch-ch-ka-ka-ka.

John Luke doesn't say anything, so you figure he can't hear it over the sound of the running water.

You step outside and squint into the woods. They seem darker than before. But the noise has stopped.

As you return to the cabin, you decide it would be a good idea to keep the machete close by. You may need it tonight.

When John Luke finishes, you head to the bathroom to clean up before bed.

But before you squeeze toothpaste on your brush, you hear the noise again.

Ch-ch-ch-ka-ka-ka.

You return to the main room and peer into the woods.

The noise definitely came from close by.

Do you run into the woods to try to find the source of the noise? Go to page 23.

Do you ignore the noise and keep getting ready for bed? Go to page 43.

TIMING IS EVERYTHING

JOHN LUKE RUSHES OUT of the dining hall ten minutes later. He's out of breath and wide-eyed and looks both amused and freaked out.

"What's going on?"

"There's trouble, Papaw Phil. I gotta get you back to the Duck Commander warehouse right away."

"What do you mean?"

"We have to save Dad and Uncle Si."

"Willie and Si?" you ask. "What have they done now?"

"It's a long story, so I'll tell you on the way. We need to go home right now."

You follow John Luke, wondering what he heard on the phone. Once you're in the Jeep, speeding away from the camp, you question him again.

"Want to explain to me what's happening?"

"Yeah. We're gonna find a time machine in the warehouse," John Luke says. "We need to open the door as soon as we can so Dad and Uncle Si can get out before it takes them back into danger."

"Are you joking with me?" you ask.

"No, sir."

"So why do we have to do this again?"

John Luke is talking so fast it takes a lot to keep up with him. You can't remember the last time you saw him this passionate and animated.

"Because right now they're in the future. And they're in big trouble."

"The *future*?"

"Yes, sir."

"That makes no sense."

"I know. But I know it's true."

"Why's that?" you ask.

"Because—because I was on the phone with this guy who had a lot of information. His name is Raymond. And he seemed to know what he was talking about."

You shake your head. "I think everyone in this state has gone *Looney Tunes* tonight."

"Yeah, I think so too," John Luke says.

He pulls up in front of the warehouse, and you both

80

hurry inside. You have no idea what's going on here, but you can't help being curious. And sure enough, right in front of you is something that looks like an outhouse.

No, that is *an outhouse.*

"John Luke—that's no time machine. It's something you use to go potty in," you tell him, just in case he's too modern to recognize it. But you have to admit, this outhouse gives you a weird feeling, like the universe is shaking around you. Maybe there's something to what John Luke is saying.

"Not this one," he says. "Trust me. It looks just like Raymond said. And we have to open it." But he hesitates for a second.

You shake your head, sigh, and let out a laugh. "Let's get this over with." You step forward and bang on the door. You've never entered an outhouse without knocking first.

There's no answer, so you pull on the handle, but the door seems to be locked.

You eye the complicated-looking control panel on the door. You start pressing random buttons and feel an electric jolt run up your arm. As the door opens, the bulb-like antennas on top of the outhouse begin flashing, and you're blinded by a bright-white light.

You have no idea what's about to happen to you.

Your story continues on page 51 in
Willie's Redneck Time Machine.

COTTON CANDY

GHOSTS AND STRANGE NOISES you can handle, but hordes of spiders? Better call for backup. Willie and Si tell John Luke they'll come as soon as they can, but who knows how long that will be.

"Let's see if the lake is covered while we wait," you suggest.

"I don't think Dad even believes me," John Luke says, pocketing his phone. "But I knew Uncle Si would be up for this."

"Wait till Willie gets here. He'll believe you then."

Snowy-white cobwebs coat the trees lining the hill on the way to the lake. As you walk along, your boots picking up lines of the sticky stuff with each step, the lake comes into view. It's entirely covered, just like you suspected it would be.

"Look at that, John Luke," you say. "God made them spiders. Can't they create pretty pictures?"

The webs shimmer in the faint wind.

"I'm tempted to dive in there," John Luke says.

"I don't know. You might want to be careful about those webs."

John Luke steps out onto the wooden dock that juts into Bluff Springs Lake. Even as he does this, he's clearing away the stringy white stuff that's covering the platform.

John Luke takes off his shirt and tosses it aside. "I'm hot."

You don't think this is such a good idea. "I'm not sure about getting in that lake."

"Dad's probably not gonna be here for another hour. It'll be cool to dive into those webs, and it looks like the spiders are all gone. But tell me if you see any more spiders coming."

He climbs onto the railing around the dock and stands.

"John Luke . . ."

"It's gonna be like jumping into the clouds! Here. Let me take a selfie."

"You and your generation with its selfies. Sounds like some kind of communicable disease. Got a bad case of the selfies."

You watch as John Luke balances himself on the wooden rail while he takes a picture of his face. Then he jumps back onto the dock and hands you his phone.

"Time to dive into some cotton candy."

He climbs up again and launches himself toward the water. He cuts through the cobwebs, making a nice round hole in the sheer covering as he splashes into the lake.

Something suddenly pops out of the water and the web covering, but it's not John Luke.

It's some kind of spider. And it's huge.

And it can walk on water—well, on the webs covering the water.

It's not just walking, though. It's streaking . . . right toward where John Luke went under.

Do you jump into the water to help John Luke?
Go to page 107.

Do you lean over the railing and scream for
him to get out of the water? Go to page 55.

HEADING OUT

"SLOW DOWN, JOHN LUKE."

Man, I should be behind the wheel. It's not that you're being overprotective. John Luke has a tendency to do things like overturn vehicles and get them spinning in the air. You have your seat belt on, but you'd rather not go spinning this evening. Especially on a full stomach.

John Luke takes his foot off the gas. The windows of his Jeep are wide-open, letting in the breeze.

"Looking forward to school starting?" you ask him.

"Not really. I was excited about working at the camp again—hope that still happens."

"What's your favorite part about it?"

"I love meeting the campers and hanging around with them. Teaching them about the Bible."

You don't need to tell your grandson he's got a good head on his shoulders and a good heart inside.

"You know," you begin, "when I was your age, all I thought about was football and girls. After hunting, of course."

You're maybe ten minutes from camp when you see a figure standing on the side of the road. He's dressed in all camo, which isn't unusual, though it's not any particular hunting season right now. His stocking cap covers long, dark hair, and he's got a beard that makes him resemble one of your family members. Over his shoulder is a backpack.

The man raises a clenched fist, sticking his thumb out to ask for a ride.

It's been a while since you've seen anybody hitchhiking. Back in the old days, it was just a part of life. If you wanted to get somewhere, you could start walking and know someone would eventually pick you up and take you the rest of the way. But these days—in these strange times full of dangerous people—you have to be careful.

John Luke slows down. "Do you know him?"

"Nope. Can't say that I do."

As you slowly pass by, both of you get a closer look at the man. His serious eyes are shrouded by his hair and beard.

"Should we pick him up?" John Luke asks.

It's getting late, and you have a place to be. But it's not like anybody's waiting on you to get there. And you always try to reach out and help people since that's what the Bible tells you to do.

But we gotta be careful.

And it's not only you in the car. You have John Luke to think about. Your grandson is no baby, but still.

It never hurts to be too careful in this world.

Do you tell John Luke to pick up the hitchhiker?
Go to page 33.

Do you tell John Luke to keep driving?
Go to page 221.

WROMBLESKERED

THIS SPIDER IS THE BIGGEST ONE you've ever seen, about the size of a plate with its crab-like legs sprawled out. John Luke is trying hard to get it off his face, but he can't do it alone. It's stuck and he's in a tricky position, lying on his back.

You take hold of its head and tug as hard as possible. But even that doesn't work at first. You have to jerk it several times before you pry it off.

Once John Luke is free, you toss the spider away, then follow it to make sure it's dead. You spend a few seconds *really* making sure it's dead.

John Luke sits in a daze. You notice a black mark on the side of his cheek.

"You okay?"

"I . . . feel . . . wrombleskered."

His eyes are looking a little wrombleskered themselves, whatever that might mean.

He's getting delirious.

"Come on." You help him to his feet.

"Mine your manners right mow."

It's like he's been poisoned with goofy juice. "Give me your keys."

"Foss the great gum," he replies.

You grab the keys from his hand and help get him into the Jeep. John Luke draws a circle in the air with his finger and mutters, "Marshies mean mean marshies."

"What kind of spider was that?" you ask, more to yourself than marshie boy.

You drive straight toward the hospital.

"Poo-poo pill," he rambles. "Did 'em jack the jake in my make?"

"Yes sir, you just lean back over there."

You want to laugh but are afraid to. Whatever's making John Luke talk crazy might also make him do something worse.

You don't worry about parking when you get to Glenwood Regional Medical Center but just leave the Jeep by the door. Someone quickly grabs a wheelchair and pushes John Luke into the hospital.

"He got bit by a spider. A *big* spider. Biggest one I've ever seen."

The aide quickly gets John Luke to an exam room, where a doctor starts to look him over.

"We's over the gooey chuckstop," John Luke informs you once you're seated inside the room.

"You're right. It was a gooey chuckstop."

Turns out it's a very good thing you got John Luke to the hospital. The doctor who's checking him tells you why.

"Every spider is different, but this one did contain a neuro-toxic venom, which means it attacks the nervous system," the doctor tells you. "I believe this bite might be similar to, but more dangerous than, that of a brown huntsman spider because its neurotoxin attacked the different ion channels. Not only that, but the venom contains high levels of serotonin, making an envenomation by this species particularly painful."

While he was talking to you, the doctor started reading from his cell phone. *Oh no.*

"Excuse me, Doctor? How do you know all this info?"

"It's right on here," he says, showing you the front of his smartphone. "Wikipedia. I wouldn't know a thing without it."

You sigh. With this doctor in charge, John Luke will probably turn into a spider any minute now. And no Wikipedia article is gonna help him then!

THE END

CABIN #3

JOHN LUKE WANTS TO CHECK OUT the "haunted" cabin, and you decide spending the night there may be the best way to prove nothing's going on after all. But no need to go inside right away. You both spend another hour beside the fire until you smell strongly of smoke. That's the beauty of being outside. You're smelling life. You're not pressing numbers on a flat screen or texting Jack and Jill about going up a hill. This is real. This is what God made you to do. To be alive and to sit down and talk.

When you finally enter the cabin with John Luke, you study the main sleeping room before brushing your teeth and washing your face.

"Looks pretty haunted to me," you whisper.

"Think so?" John Luke takes a step back.

"Yep. I mean, you see all those kids, right? Lying in their bunks?"

John Luke shakes his head. Of course he's just looking at a rectangular room full of empty bunk beds in rows.

"Are you sure? You sure you don't see them?"

"No, sir." He appears both concerned and confused.

"I guess I'm the only one who sees dead people then."

You both laugh.

John Luke takes a bottom bunk in the corner of the room, while you take the bunk right next to his. There's a window by your beds that now only reveals darkness.

It takes a while for you to fall asleep. The bunk is not nearly as big or comfortable as your bed. Plus, there's no Miss Kay right next to you. But John Luke's steady breathing makes it clear that he's already out.

You're nearly asleep when an abrupt tapping sound jolts you up. You wonder if you're dreaming, but the crunching of the less-than-cozy mattress reminds you where you are.

The tapping continues—more of a knocking than a tapping, actually. You realize it's coming from the door to the cabin.

You're not sure what time it is, but it has to be after midnight.

Tap-tap-tap.

Now it's even louder.

Someone is at the door. And the way they're knocking, they really want to get inside.

But it's not even locked. Why don't they try the handle?

Do you open the door? Go to page 9.

Do you ignore the knocking and figure it
will eventually stop? Go to page 157.

SILENCE

THERE'S A STRANGE SORT OF STILLNESS over the camp. You remember the times you've come here to share God's Word and speak to the campers about Jesus. They'd usually be pretty quiet when you were talking, but nothing like this. Right now there are no kids. There are only shadows. But you and John Luke wander around, hoping to find someone who can shed more light on the situation.

"Let's go check if Jeffrey is here," John Luke suggests.

Jeffrey is one of the regular employees who lives in a small RV on the grounds. He's a cook and an electrician and a janitor and a little bit of everything. You head over to his silver aluminum RV and knock on the door.

John Luke peers through a window. "I don't think he's in there."

"Is he on vacation or something?"

"Maybe he took off since everybody else is gone." John Luke steps away from the RV. "You believe in ghosts?"

"I believe in angels and demons and spiritual warfare. But as far as the Ghosts of Christmas Past, Present, and Future visiting me anytime soon? Uh-uh. Nope." You know the kids around camp love ghost stories. What camper doesn't enjoy a spooky tale told around a campfire at night? But those are just tales. They're fun stories to freak you out. Especially when you listen to them in the dark woods, with the creatures of the night watching you in the pitch-black. . . . You glance around nervously before following John Luke once more. The two of you head for the gym.

John Luke hits the lights. "They've redone the floor."

You find a basketball and dribble it a couple times. "Once upon a time your grandfather could shoot some hoops. Football was always my sport, but I played some basketball too." You take a shot but miss.

Before you can retrieve the basketball and try for another shot, you notice a feather on the floor and pick it up. "What's this from?"

John Luke takes it and shakes his head. "I'm not sure."

"If you ask me, it looks like it came from some kind of Indian headdress or something."

"Maybe it's from Chief Stinkum."

You stare at John Luke. "What in the world are you talking about?"

"Haven't you heard Dad tell the story? The ghost story about Chief Stinkum?"

"Think I missed that boat."

"It changes every time he tells it. I like the Zodie Sims story better."

"Maybe there's too much imagination happening around here," you say. "That's why kids are getting crazy ideas."

John Luke holds up the feather. "This has to belong to someone."

"I guess so. But there's nothing else to see in this gym. I think it's time to keep moving."

Do you head toward the lake? Go to page 167.

**Do you look a little longer for someone
to talk to? Go to page 193.**

**Do you go back to the Jeep to get your stuff
and put it in one of the cabins? Go to page 7.**

MOMMY

YOU GRAB THE GLOVES from the backseat of John Luke's Jeep. The knife, you remember, is in the rear.

The good thing about the Robertson family is there's always some kind of hunting tool floating around, ready to be used.

You put on the gloves and dart over to get the spider off John Luke. You grab it with one hand and attack it with the knife in your other hand, careful not to stick your grandson.

Just as you free John Luke and stomp on the spider, you spot something at the doorway to one of the cabins.

The spider you killed must've been Big Sis, and it looks like Mommy is still alive.

She's alive and very angry.

The legs of the big spider that jumped on John Luke look *half* the size of the legs on this one. If that last spider was the size of a plate, this is the size of a copy machine. It's gargantuan.

It's also so fast it looks like it can sprint.

The spider is on you before you have a chance to move your arm. You try to use the knife but miss and somehow drop the knife by your side.

"Papaw Phil!" John Luke shouts.

Then everything happens in slow motion.

You

try

to

open

your

mouth

but

when

you

do

all

you

can

say

is

a

very

slow

"Nooooooooooooooooooooooooooooooooooooooooooooooo!"

And somewhere in the middle of that long, drawn-out "noooooooooooooooooooooooooooooooooooooooooooo" that just keeps going and going and going, you hear something behind you.

A door opening and shutting.

Boots stomping.

And a blast of gunfire.

The spider explodes in a big, gooey burst of yuck. You turn to see who fired the gun.

It's Jase.

Behind him you see a wooden outhouse. One that's got antennas on it and some kind of computer panel on the front. It looks vaguely familiar, somehow.

Jase pats you on the back. "Hey, Dad. Just looking out for you guys."

Jase is wearing all camo and his trademark black hat.

"How'd you know to come here?"

"That thing over there—the outhouse. I was told I needed to come to this particular moment in time and save you."

You don't even know where to begin.

Jase nods and runs back to the outhouse. "I'll see you later."

"Where are you going?"

"I gotta go back to where I came from. Still got some things to do."

Nothing Jase is saying is making sense.

"What *are* you talking about, Son?"

He opens the door. "I got two words for you: *box set*."

Then he steps inside, and in seconds the outhouse disappears. *Not possible.* Jase is going to have some explaining to do when you get home.

John Luke stares at the remains of the two dead spiders next to his feet.

"I hope those are the biggest ones," he says as he steps around them.

"Considering how this day is going, anything is possible," you remind him. "Anything."

For the moment, you don't see any more spiders—at least no more big ones like those two you guys just killed.

You decide you've seen enough spiders and webs for the day. It's time to leave the camp and call for reinforcements.

You're not giving up. But you know when enough's enough.

You and John Luke will be back. Very soon.

THE END

RIDE 'EM, COWBOY

THE GOOD NEWS: you're brave enough to jump into Bluff Springs Lake.

The bad news: instead of diving into the water to get to John Luke, you end up landing on the back of the spider as it dashes past.

You don't get off, though—you decide you might as well ride the sucker. It can't bite you if you're up here . . . you hope not, anyway.

This spider looks more like some kind of mutant crab, with long, spiky legs and pinchers. Even with your weight on it, the spider doesn't sink.

You hold on more tightly as the spider scurries away from John Luke, toward the shore. As it arrives on the rocks and dirt, it stops abruptly and you get bolted off to one side. You nearly land on your head and topple across the ground. The spider continues toward the woods, then seems to change its mind. It stops and begins walking toward you again, slower this time.

You wish you had your gun. Or your knife. Or any kind of weapon. But you don't have a thing.

You're stuck and you're about to be attacked by a massive monster spider, and all you have are your bare hands.

I can still take that creature on.

It seems to pause for a moment, perhaps readying itself to attack. You get to your feet and prepare to strike back at the thing. Then a gun blast goes off.

It's the sound of a shotgun. The round body of the spider explodes just in time.

You look behind you and see John Luke emerging from the water. But he's not holding a gun.

"That's what I call hitting the bull's-eye, Jack!"

Si is standing on the hill above the lake, shotgun in hand. "What in the world are you mermaids doing swimming in the lake with that thing?"

You walk up to the motionless spider. "You ever seen a bug this big?"

"Yeah, sure." Si nods. "There were some big ones over in Vietnam."

"They weren't like this."

"Hey, look, they were even bigger. We had to use helicopters to take them down." Then he starts humming *Ride of the Valkyries*. "Ta-dah-dah-dah-dah-dah, dah-dah-dah-*dah*-dah, dah-dah-dah-*dah*-dah, dah-dah-dah-dah."

Now John Luke is standing next to you.

You glare at him. "Told you not to go in the water."

"Thanks for jumping on the spider. That was cool."

"I was trying to help you. I didn't think I'd be riding a bull spider."

"I heard this place had a few cobwebs around," Si says.

"Just a few," you tell him.

"Good thing I brought my shotgun."

You poke one of the spider's long legs. "Ever eaten giant spider legs?"

"I hope that's the last one we run into," John Luke says.

Si clears his throat. "I hope I never see another spider in my life."

You agree with your brother. You've done your part out here. Maybe you'll finally call animal control and let them take over.

THE END

GREAT & WHITE

THESE COMMERCIALS SURE ARE BORING, and this recliner sure is cozy . . .

Next thing you know, a banging sound wakes you up. You feel a slight breeze on your face. The door must be open. You let your eyes adjust and squint across the room at John Luke's bed.

It's empty.

What's he up to now?

Maybe he's taking a midnight stroll. Nothing wrong with that. Unless this place really is haunted, in which case things could get bad. But neither you nor John Luke are worried about anything like that . . . well, not too worried. Just in case, you pull yourself out of your chair and go outside to see where he might be.

Maybe he sneaked outside to talk to a girl . . . but you thought all the girls went home.

Maybe he can't sleep, and he's thinking and praying.

You stand right outside the cabin door and listen, but you don't hear anything, so you consider your options. There are three main places for kids at the camp, if you remember right: the cabins, the gym, and the lake. The lights are off in the gym, and the boys' cabins are silent. So you decide to try the lake.

By the time you walk the wooded path to the top of the small hill that leads down to the water, you hear something besides the familiar sound of the small waterfall nearby.

Someone splashing.

Did John Luke sneak a girl down to the lake to swim with?

You think you know the answer, but then again, you remember when you were a teenager. If you had some more smarts and soul back then, you would've saved yourself a lot of trouble later on. But you can't go back in time, can you?

Unless you spot an outhouse time machine in the middle of the . . . Oh, never mind.

When you get closer to the water, the nearly full moon reflecting on its surface, you confirm that only one figure's swimming in it. John Luke's head bobs up and down as he cuts through the still waters.

You step onto the dock that juts into the lake.

John Luke flips over and splashes with his legs. You laugh as you watch him, figuring he couldn't sleep and was maybe just hot. You're feeling kinda warm yourself.

You glance up at the sky and stare at the moon for a moment. Beautiful. Then you spot something in the water. Something breaking the smooth surface.

Something other than John Luke.

You squint, trying to bring it into focus.

I need more light.

Your eyes are playing tricks on you. Surely.

But a steady wake is coming across the lake, closer and closer. It's making a straight line toward John Luke.

And you swear there's a fin sticking out of the water. Like a shark fin.

But that's crazy.

It's still coming nearer, faster.

"Hey, John Luke," you call.

But you know he can't hear you. And this has gotta be the moonlight and the shadowy lake playing tricks on you.

But no . . . it's closer now.

Something even stranger is happening too. Because with every inch of progress the shape makes, you feel your heart turn over with a trembling, booming beat.

Daaauh.

Daaauh.

Daaauh.

Daaauh daaauh.

Daaauh daaauh daaauh daaauh.

Bombombombombombombombombom.

You get the idea.

You know how this is going to end.

"John Luke!" you shout, urgent now.

But he still hasn't seen you, still can't hear. Still has no idea he's being chased by a shark.

My heartbeat is becoming stronger, faster. Or is that actually music?

"John Luke, get out of the water! The music is louder—get out!"

But he's oblivious.

"John Luke, come on. Listen—don't you hear it? It's John Williams—can't you hear? Get out! Get out now!"

The volume of the music keeps increasing.

Where's this music coming from?

The fin has almost caught up to John Luke.

Hasn't it been moving across the lake for a long time? I mean, shouldn't this scene be over now?

Bigger, stronger, faster, wilder.

More tuba. More tuba!

And then.

Then.

No.

No!

(Keep playing, orchestra!)

Faster—faster—faster.

Noooooooooooooo.

You wipe the sweat off your forehead, scream, and then . . .

You're in front of the little cabin television. It's a late-night showing of *Jaws*.

A fan blows on your face, and your bare feet are propped up in the recliner. Other than the muted sound of the television, you can't hear anything. John Luke is secure in his bed.

But your heart is racing as quickly as before.

You could've sworn you were just out by the lake. . . .

But you're here now. Which is a good thing.

Maybe, though, to be on the safe side, you'll discuss this dream with John Luke in the morning. Just to give him a helpful warning. About being careful next time he goes swimming. And watching out for unusual animals.

Especially ones with fins.

As long as your imagination doesn't get the better of you again, you'll be prepared to resume this investigation in the morning. But maybe you'll save the lake for last.

THE END

AN INSANE ODYSSEY

YOU RETRIEVE THE AX from the cabin and hold it in front of you, ready to cut off a tail. Ready to engage in hand-to-hand combat.

Some might say you're old, but your brain still works at optimal level. People don't understand. Behind this beard and these camo pants is a man capable of keeping up with Jason Bourne.

Age is all in your head. And in my head, I'm still twenty-seven. Active and kicking.

You approach the sounds. And the closer you get, the more they start to change.

At first, they suggest some kind of animal gnawing down a tree in the wilderness. But then suddenly you hear something different.

"Can you make me some coffee?" Miss Kay's voice says.

You stop and turn around in the forest.

What in the world?

You keep walking until you hear another voice.

"Those ducks are coming any second now."

That was Si talking, as if the two of you are in a duck blind this very instant.

You slow down, the ax ready for whatever lies ahead. You notice a strange blue glow in the woods.

"Aw, come on," a voice says. "Everybody knows you gotta send out a decoy first."

That's definitely Jase.

You move forward like you're in a dream. Different voices talking to you from all around.

"Yeah, I think it's gonna be fine."

That's Mac Owen, one of your best friends. Is he visiting from Colorado?

What's going on? Am I dreaming?

The voices continue, and the cold blue glow gets progressively brighter until you climb a hill and see where the light is coming from.

There's some kind of black shape that appears to be floating in the middle of the woods.

You hold the ax steady, ready to strike. But this isn't an animal. It's something you've never seen.

It's one of those times where you stumble onto something that you just look at and go, *Huh?* with your mouth open.

Well, your mouth may be hanging open, but it's hidden in your beard.

The black object that's hanging there looks a lot like . . .

You get closer.

It doesn't look like one—it is *one.*

It's a duck call.

A gigantic black floating duck call, like nothing you've seen on Earth.

This thing seems to draw you closer. You keep walking toward it.

Then you hear Elton John singing "Rocket Man." No, not Elton John. This singer has a terrible voice . . . and he doesn't seem to know the lyrics. *Si?*

You don't know what's happening. But there must be a bigger meaning here. Another picture. A different story. A different book, even.

You keep walking ahead, step by step. You drop the ax and hold out your hand.

You can't imagine that this thing has anything to do with the strange goings-on at the camp. But you need to find the truth behind this hovering, hulking duck call in the middle of nowhere.

It might be time to move to book three.

THE END

STANLEY CUP
PLAY-OFFS

YOU WAIT WITH JOHN LUKE IN SILENCE until it's been so long that the chainsaw man has to be gone. You're not frightened. Nah. Around these parts, crazy situations make people do crazy things. You've seen it all. Maybe that chainsaw-wielding madman just needs a hug.

"I think we should take off now," you tell John Luke.

"In my Jeep?"

You give him a big thumbs-down. "No. Too loud. Hmm . . ." The hitchhiker you met earlier crosses your mind. "Let's take the woods to the main road. Then try to see about flagging down a ride."

It takes about half an hour to hike to the main road. You don't see or hear any more from the chainsaw guy.

"What do you think that dude was trying to do?" John Luke asks.

"Usually when someone is trying to break into my house with a chainsaw, I don't stick around to ask," you tell him. "I'm pretty sure he wasn't there to sell Girl Scout cookies."

You've just started walking down the road when you see the lights from an approaching car. Both you and John Luke wave it down with wild arm gestures.

"We'll get him to take us to the police station," you tell John Luke.

It's a good idea.

Until you see the driver.

He's wearing a hockey mask. And it's not even hockey season.

That's not the only problem.

He's got friends.

"Uh, you know what?" you say. "I think we're okay on foot."

But the doors all open, and you realize there's a whole hockey team getting out of the car.

"John Luke, go!" you shout.

You run as fast as you can on John Luke's heels, weaving through the woods until you lose these guys. Come to think of it, walking home on the back roads might be a better plan after all—no matter how long it takes. This will be some story to tell the police.

THE END

I CAN'T BELIEVE
IT'S BUTTER

A BREEZE WAKES YOU UP. It takes you a minute to remember you're at the camp, sleeping on a bunk bed. As your eyes adjust, you notice that the front door to the cabin is open. Then you turn your head and realize John Luke's bed is empty.

He must have gone outside for some reason.

He's sleepwalking.

This is a truth about John Luke that nobody knows except his family. Yes, he sleepwalks. But it's not normal sleepwalking. Sometimes the sleepwalking lasts for days. His entire sophomore year of high school was spent in one big sleepwalk. It took well-paid professionals to revive him that time.

Now he only awakens to the phrase *Butter on a biscuit.*

But he obviously has to be within hearing range for this phrase to work.

"John Luke?" You search the cabin in case he's still here. "Butter on a biscuit."

But he's nowhere.

You sigh, putting on some clothes and trudging outside.

"Butter on a biscuit!" you shout. No need to keep it down—there's not a soul around to hear you. Surely you'd sound like a crazy person screaming about biscuits, but then again John Luke probably *looks* like a crazy person walking around in his pajamas in the middle of the night.

"Butter on a biscuit!"

You listen carefully. Nothing.

You better head to the lake just to make sure he's not swimming while asleep. You're not sure how sleepwalking works exactly, but it might be dangerous to go sleepswimming. Who knows.

One time John Luke went out on a sleepwalking date with a girl from school. Every time she spoke, he just nodded and said funny things like "I love bacon." She assumed he was being goofy. But when he dropped her off and she said goodbye, he said, "I'll miss you, Clarise." That wasn't the girl's name, so she got upset. John Luke later had to explain he was sleepwalking the whole time.

For some reason, she didn't believe him.

As you make your way down the hill toward the water, you hear someone singing. It takes you a minute to register that it's John Luke.

He's dancing on the dock and acting like he's holding a microphone.

What in the world? This is a new symptom.

John Luke doesn't notice you walking toward the "stage."

"'Oh, oh,'" he shouts. "'That's what makes you beautiful.'"

You smile. "Thank you, John Luke. I feel beautiful."

He keeps singing and dancing, and you can't help but watch for a moment. Then you call out, "Butter on a biscuit," and he snaps to.

"Papaw Phil," he says, looking around him in confusion. "Was I . . . ?"

"Yep."

John Luke steps off the dock, stumbling a bit. "Was I singing and . . . ?"

"Yep."

"Did anybody else . . . ?"

"Nope." You rest a hand on his shoulder, trying not to laugh. "Your secret is safe with me."

The free John Luke concert is over. For tonight, anyway.

John Luke's antics are the only strange sights or sounds you find at the camp that night. You'll just have to tell Isaiah his "ghost" never showed up.

THE END

FREAK OUT

"JOHN LUKE, YOU BETTER GO INTO THE CABIN and wait for me."

"What was that?" he asks.

"I don't know, but I'm going to find out."

"I can go with you."

"Yes, you could, but I think it's best you stay here."

John Luke doesn't argue, even though the look on his face tells you he thinks it's a bad idea.

"You have your cell, right?" you ask. "You call the cops if something funny happens."

"Somebody was just screaming in the woods," John Luke says. "That's not funny?"

"If something *else* happens. While I'm gone."

"Like if I hear you scream?"

Good point.

"I won't be screaming. You won't hear that." You pause and think for a moment. "And if I'm not back in an hour, then get out of here, okay?"

Now John Luke looks like he *really* thinks this is a bad idea.

You watch him head to the cabin and shut the door before you venture into the darkness, in the direction of the scream.

The farther into the forest you get, the more pitch-black it becomes.

You hear branches cracking ahead like someone's running off.

An owl makes its hooting call somewhere behind you. The nightly sounds of the Louisiana wilderness surround you.

Then another *ch-ch-ch-ka-ka-ka* seems to whisper to you. You grasp the handle of your machete.

More tree limbs snap and break, but this time you can't tell where they are.

You hear something right behind you and turn around. "John Luke? Is that you? If that's you, tell me now."

Nothing.

The darkness of the woods doesn't frighten you, nor do the strange sounds. The scariest thing would be if something happened to John Luke. And you want to keep yourself safe too.

Miss Kay would get upset if I didn't make it home.

You retrace your steps. Then you notice something through the trees in front of you that looks like a fire.

It *is* a fire. But it's too big to be the campfire you just came from.

Oh no. One of the cabins must be on fire.

John Luke.

You run through the woods like you haven't run in twenty-five years. You see flames consuming the cabin John Luke just entered. You can detect the scent of gasoline all around you.

You know someone did this on purpose.

A part of you almost dives into the flames because you don't see John Luke. At first.

But then you notice the figure in the driver's seat of the Jeep. It's him.

You rush over to the vehicle and try the door, but it's locked. John Luke jumps and turns to you. He opens the door, but you can tell something's wrong.

Does John Luke start rambling about a disturbing encounter from his childhood? What does this have to do with the fire? (There's a connection—promise.) Go to page 211.

Does John Luke tell you he knows how the fire started? (Finally, a chance to learn the truth.) Go to page 59.

Does John Luke confess to something you can hardly believe? (This is going to be good!) Go to page 151.

28 MINUTES LATER

YOU HEAD BACK HOME ON FOOT. This situation is desperate! But when you finally get there, your front door's broken down. Miss Kay is nowhere to be found.

It's happening too fast. The nightmare is too real.

Cue the music from your favorite suspenseful movie. 'Cause this is how the world ends.

John Luke—or whatever was left of him as the allibeaver venom took hold of his system—apparently knew he needed help and drove toward the first place he could think of: home.

By the time he got there, the transformation was complete, and he instantly infected his whole family.

They, in turn, infected their entire neighborhood.

Before you were even back from the camp, West Monroe was mostly gone.

And that's how it starts.

Once you realize that you're alone in this town and everyone else has turned into allibeavers, you take up the defense, loading John Luke's Jeep with guns, ammunition, and food.

You start hearing reports on the radio. People all over the state are beginning to realize that something weird is happening. *Something* is on the attack, but no one yet understands what it is. Strange, conflicting reports communicate only partial truths.

You try over and over to call the family members who are still human, as far as you know. Finally you get a message on your answering machine from Alan.

"They're gone, Dad! Something's happening! I don't know—I'm the last one who hasn't changed. Maybe it's because I don't have a beard. I'm not sure. But they're trying to break into the house. They're coming—you guys gotta get out of there fast! They're—"

The line goes dead.

You know what that means.

You've seen zombie movies and end-of-the-world movies.

But you've also seen Jason Bourne movies.

In this case, you're Jason Bourne, and the rest of the world is full of zombies. Or . . . well, allibeavers.

There's no time to grieve. You have to act.

You have to take care of yourself.

You have to stay clear of trouble.

It's time to head for the safest place you can think of in the event of an allibeaver outbreak.

You make a phone call and get his voice mail.

"Mac, this is Phil. I'm driving to your place. Keep an eye on the news. Be careful. Stay away from anything that resembles an alligator. Or a beaver. I'll explain everything when I get there."

You start driving to the Owens' house.

Divide, Colorado, is a long ways away from Louisiana. And hopefully from the allibeavers.

But you know you'll be secure there.

Mac's one of the original Duck Commanders.

You all gotta stick together when the end of the world comes.

THE END

ALFRED HITCHCOCK'S
THE DUCKS

JOHN LUKE IS STILL GROGGY as you both stand at the doorway, preparing to exit the cabin. You told him about the ducks, but he doesn't understand the magnitude of what awaits you two outside. You give him a nod.

"Okay. Here we go."

The door opens. You put an arm around John Luke and guide him outside.

There are more ducks now than there were only minutes ago. And it's not just mallards, either. There are all kinds. Even some that you've never seen around here.

Some that don't belong here at all.

There's a white-cheeked pintail. A king eider. A blue-winged teal. A surf scoter.

The ducks are covering the camp. They're on the ground and in the trees.

In the trees?

They're on the benches outside and all over the cabins. They're banging into each other because there are literally thousands. Tens of thousands? Hundreds of thousands?

As you lead John Luke out, he starts shaking his head and resisting.

"No," he says. Then, louder, "No, no!"

"It's okay," you say, your arm still around him. "We'll be fine."

"I know. But why are you acting like I can't walk?" he asks.

"Oh. Sorry. Just helpin'."

Side by side, you move slowly through the sea of ducks, careful not to enrage them. You don't want them suddenly attacking. This many of anything would take you down. They might just all try to land on you at once and suffocate the life out of you.

John Luke accidentally kicks a duck in the head.

"Easy," you whisper. "We have to make it to the Jeep."

There are ducks all over the vehicle too. It's like a snow-storm with ducks instead of snowflakes. You have to shoo away ducks from the windshield and the roof.

Once inside the Jeep, you're both too stunned to talk. John Luke starts the engine.

"How'd this happen?" he finally asks.

You shake your head. *No idea.*

You don't know if this duck infestation is only affecting the camp or if it's happening in other places too.

What about the rest of West Monroe? What about all of Louisiana?

You turn on the radio but don't hear anything out of the ordinary.

"Let's go to your house," you suggest.

"Think Dad will know what's happening?"

"No, of course not. But Willie will have a plan. He's always got a plan."

John Luke slowly begins driving, letting the ducks move out of the way. They cover the drive all the way to the main road you take to exit the camp.

The ducks have revolted.

Not only that . . .

They've multiplied.

And you're sneaking away in the night. This time the ducks are winning.

Yeah. Some Duck Commander *you've* turned out to be.

The worst part is, you haven't even solved the mystery. Could the ducks be responsible for the strange happenings around here? It's possible. But it's not like they're planning to confess anytime soon.

Wait . . . ducks can't confess! They can't even talk. I must be starting to quack up.

THE END

THE SCENT OF MYSTERY

YOU IMMEDIATELY APPROACH THE POLICE, but the officer in charge asks you to take a seat and wait until they can sort things out.

An hour later, with the fire extinguished after the firemen tried to salvage whatever they could of the burning cabin, a cop walks toward you. You're sitting at a picnic table with John Luke and Willie, who arrived about thirty minutes ago.

"You guys know anything about this?"

He hands you a glass bottle that's shaped like a duck. You look at it and notice it's filled with liquid and has a spray top.

"I know what that is," Willie says, taking the bottle from you. "It's a cologne some guy was trying to brand with Duck Commander. He was callin' it 'Duck Scent.' Where'd you find this?"

"It was in the field—a few bottles of it," the cop says.

"That guy was carrying a backpack full of something," you say.

"I wonder if it's the nut job who tried to sell this to us," Willie says.

"What was wrong with it?" you ask.

Willie sprays it a few times so you can get a nice good sniff. It smells rancid, like someone died.

Then you remember smelling something like that before. *When John Luke and I picked up the hitchhiker.*

Could it be he wasn't covered in body odor, but rather was wearing the never-to-be-released Duck Commander Duck Scent cologne?

"How can somethin' smell so bad?" you ask.

"That's awful," John Luke says, coughing.

"We're gonna want to get the name of the guy trying to sell you this stuff," the cop informs Willie.

"Absolutely," Willie says. "That guy always seemed suspicious."

"No," the policeman says. "Not because of that. I wanna know how I can buy my own bottle of Duck Scent cologne!"

THE END

STAYING HOME

WHATEVER'S GOING ON AT THAT CAMP can surely wait till you've had a good night's rest. John Luke decides to spend the night at your house so the two of you can drive over first thing tomorrow morning. The Egyptian Ratscrew game finally ends, but everybody takes their time leaving. You wind up going to bed at a later hour than usual and fall asleep in about ten seconds.

A high-pitched scream wakes you.

"What was that?" you mutter to Miss Kay, who is already awake and looking out the window.

"Sounds like some kind of animal."

It's unlike any animal you've ever heard. It reminds you a bit of the nasally, braying noise of a mule, but it's much higher. And it lasts much longer.

"Maybe it'll stop in a minute," Miss Kay says, climbing back into bed.

"It better be stoppin' in a minute."

If there's one thing in this world you don't like, it's being woken up. The kids and the grandkids have always known that. It takes a lot to wake you, and if something or someone does, they better watch out.

After about five minutes, you realize you're going to have to get out there and deal with this. Being woken up is one thing, but being forced from your bed is another.

This is gonna be the last sound that animal ever makes.

You put on some clothes and shoes, then head toward the front door.

The room where John Luke is sleeping is quiet, so you leave him alone. He's a heavy sleeper like you and the rest of the Robertson boys. And you're sure you can handle this creature yourself.

You grab a rifle and a flashlight and silently open the door. The outdoor lights are on, illuminating the yard. As you shut the door behind you, the sound stops. You step in the direction the noise came from, but everything is quiet.

As you venture down a trail into the woods, you keep waiting for the sound to start up again. For a second, you stop and listen.

Nothing.

The worst part is you're wide-awake now. This is why you don't like to be woken up. Once it happens, it's almost impossible to go back to sleep.

The bushes ahead of you rustle, and then you hear the sound again. It's louder out here. You aim the high-powered flashlight toward it but don't see anything. You walk closer, the annoying clamor louder than ever. But nothing appears unusual.

After searching for about twenty minutes, with the strange noise coming and going, you see bushes shake and hear branches snap as if something large is moving around. But you still can't see whatever it is.

Just like that, all the noises stop. The animal that was making this eerie sound—no trace of it.

Well, that's weird.

You know it's gotta be close—maybe only a few feet from you, using the cloak of darkness as its camo.

You're not sure whether to stay outside until you find it or to go back inside and try getting some sleep.

Do you stay outside? Go to page 71.

Do you go inside? Go to page 231.

SLASHER

YOU FEEL SOMETHING WARM against your cheek. You're deep in sleep, but this sensation—it's strange. It's almost like someone's standing over you, watching you, breathing on you. A person with hot breath and a cold heart.

Something scrapes along your bed.

You open your eyes with a jolt and scan the room.

No hot breath or cold heart to be seen. Surely you were just dreaming.

Then you hear mumbling from the bed next to you.

"I didn't . . . No, it moved—I didn't hit it. . . . The tree hit the Jeep."

It's only John Luke talking in his sleep.

"A hundred trees—mean trees—flipped the Jeep. . . . Bad tree."

You decide to leave your talking grandson and head to the bathroom. There are many good things about getting older, but these nightly trips are not one of them.

As you're washing your hands, you hear something outside. A branch cracking. You don't think it's anything to worry about, but then you hear a few more cracks.

May as well open the door and peer outside. For a moment you don't see anything but darkness. But then something white and oval-shaped approaches you.

More branches snap. The sound of footsteps can be heard. Running footsteps.

The white thing gets closer and closer until you can finally tell what it is.

It's a white mask. With black eyes and a tiny nose and mouth.

Someone's *wearing* the white mask and running toward you.

Close the door. Get back inside.

When the masked stranger is five feet from the cabin, you slam the door and hear a loud bang. You crack the door open, revealing the figure sprawled on the ground.

"Are you crazy?" you shout, stepping on the guy's chest so he can't move.

You assume it's a guy because the person is big and tall. He's also wearing camo.

Wait a minute.

You loom over him, hoping you appear intimidating and not scared at all. *Not at all.*

"Take off the mask," you command. You let him stand, but he doesn't remove the disguise. "I said take it off. Who are you?"

He pulls off his creepy white Halloween mask to reveal . . . a dark, thick beard and long hair. He looks just like the guy you passed on the road earlier this evening.

"Were you hitchhiking out there?"

His eyes don't move. He simply nods.

"What do you think you're doing? What's going on with the creepy mask?"

He just laughs.

"You think this is funny? I got a kid inside here. The police wouldn't think it's too funny."

He keeps laughing. Then his smile turns grim.

"They're coming," he whispers.

"They're coming? Who's coming?"

He turns, and suddenly you see them. Several—no, make that a dozen figures emerging from the dark.

Wait a minute. Where'd this fog come from?

They're all wearing masks like his.

"Is this some kind of joke?" you ask.

The man keeps laughing. And you decide enough's enough. You shut the door and lock it behind you.

You wake up John Luke and tell him to call

Willie or the cops—or anybody—but he doesn't have cell service.

And you keep thinking, *This is a joke. This is a joke.* But it's no joke at all.

The hitchhiker's voice reaches you from outside. "You should have picked me up."

Go to page 189.

FAMILY RESEMBLANCE

YOU CRAWL BACK INTO BED and pull the covers over your head. *Wait till I tell John Luke about this nightmare in the morning.*

A crashing sound wakes you up. You open your eyes but see only darkness.

Somebody's gonna pay for that noise.

You crawl out of bed, thinking again about your crazy nightmare. Alligators and beavers and John Luke and . . .

There's the crashing sound again.

"It's the middle of the night, and whoever's making all that ruckus better zip it!" you shout out the window. Then you open the door, deciding a face-to-face confrontation might work best.

There in your cabin entryway stands a terrifying creature—a creature you thought existed only in your wildest dreams.

You pinch yourself to make sure you're not still sleeping. *Ouch.*

The thing has a beaver tail and a long alligator snout with sharp teeth. It appears to be grinning.

Yes. It's an allibeaver.

You notice that this particular allibeaver is wearing a bandanna.

A stars-and-stripes bandanna.

Willie's bandanna.

Oh no. John Luke must have gone home and infected his family. Now Willie's here to get you. You wish you had an ax handy to cut off his tail and stop the madness.

As he charges you, you think about how much Willie's always resembled an allibeaver in some ways.

THE END OF THE "TAIL"

TIME AFTER TIME

"WE WERE ALREADY HERE ONCE," John Luke says as you join him in the Jeep, the walls of the cabin crashing down amid the fire.

"John Luke, what are you talking about?"

"This place . . . this cabin. It will be the site of a crime in the future. And because of that, it must be destroyed."

"Son—did you eat too many fried pickles tonight?"

He gets out of the Jeep, his forehead dotted with sweat. You follow him.

"I had to make it right," he says.

"What do you mean?"

John Luke is out of breath as if he's been running laps for the last hour.

"I went into the bathroom, and then I saw it. Some kind of . . . outhouse. Right inside the cabin. It seemed really familiar—I'm not sure why. I got inside the outhouse, and then . . . something happened. I was transported to the future. And I saw a kid being bullied in this cabin."

"So *you* did this?" You can't believe it.

"It's the only way. This kid I saw getting bullied—it only happens here, in cabin one. It won't happen if the cabin's not here. I mean, it won't be the same in cabin two. Right?"

You shake your head. "This doesn't make any sense."

"I know—exactly. It's mind-boggling, right?"

"No, John Luke. It's just plain dumb."

He looks at you. "Your mind's not boggled?"

"No. Not at all. But yours, I'm thinking, might possibly be. We need to get you to a doctor, and fast."

You're about to drive John Luke to the hospital in West Monroe when you see it blocking your way. A wooden rectangular shape standing in the driveway leading out of the camp.

It's an outhouse.

A strange-looking outhouse.

You look at John Luke, and then you head toward it.

You're gonna go back in time and undo what he just did. Why not?

Even if you can't change John Luke's actions, you bet time travel will be pretty fun. Fun enough to write a whole book about it, maybe.

THE END

A CASE OF LYCANTHROPY (A REALLY BIG WORD FOR A BIG CHANGE)

"SO WHAT'D THE THING LOOK LIKE?"

John Luke is driving you to the hospital in his Jeep. Miss Kay helped clean and bandage your arm a few minutes ago. The bite was pretty deep—whatever sort of animal did this to you, it had big enough teeth to take off a chunk of your arm.

"I didn't see much of it, to be honest. But it had to be a wolf." *What else could it be? A werewolf? A big, angry, oversize German shepherd?*

"I haven't ever seen a wolf around here," John Luke says.

"I've never encountered one that big anywhere. Or that annoying soundin'."

A pain rips through your arm. It feels hot—exactly like a searing burn, as if you're resting your forearm on a grill that's been cooking steaks for the past half hour. You tighten your fist and grit your teeth.

"You okay, Papaw Phil?" John Luke asks.

He must've heard you grunt.

"Oh yeah. Just a tad bit sore."

You start to sweat and feel light-headed. You took a couple Advil, but now you know this is more serious.

"I think I might need some help once I'm at the hospital," you tell John Luke.

The headlights piercing the dark country road begin to blur and blend. You see weird things in your head.

Packs of wild dogs . . . the countryside . . . the full blue moon . . .

The blackness of the night fills your head. You shake it and try to stay awake. "I'm feeling kinda dizzy."

John Luke speeds up.

The burning continues, this time throughout your whole body.

Then something else happens. Your shoes feel too small. Your jeans too tight. Your shirt too snug.

It's like you're about to explode, to rip right out of your clothes.

Something's happening—something bad. I'm changing. What's goin' on here?

You turn to John Luke and get this weird, awful sort of feeling.

You're hungry.

You glance down at your hand and see that it's become a paw. A wolf paw with long, sharp claws.

You want to scream but can't.

But that's okay because John Luke does it for you.

It's the last thing you remember before the transformation is complete.

THE HOWLING END

DREAMING AND HAUNTING

WHOEVER'S TAPPING AT THE DOOR CAN WAIT.

And if *that's* what's freaking out campers in the middle of the night, then maybe you need to talk to kids these days about having some guts and backbone. There's nothing haunting about the tapping. It's annoying, but you ignore it and soon fall into a deep slumber.

For a while you dream of groundhogs. You have no idea what inspired this dream, but you find yourself at a campfire with several of the rodents. The first odd thing is that they can all talk. The second thing is their size—they're as big as humans (and they're sitting upright like you are too). The third and weirdest detail is that they all sound like your sons.

There's the biggest groundhog, who thinks he's the boss of the rest of them. His name is Weehog.

Then there's a short groundhog who acts like a big baby. His name is Jep-hog.

The third one is really talkative with a bit of a dramatic flair. His name is Jayhog.

And the fourth is a groundhog who doesn't have any hair. His name is Al-hog.

Of course, since this is a dream and all your sons have suddenly become groundhogs, you have no idea what's going to happen next. But just as Weehog is starting to tell a story, you hear a crash and a boom.

You open your eyes but don't see any groundhogs. You realize you're back in the cabin at Camp Ch-Yo-Ca.

Is it haunting time yet?

John Luke stirs in the bed beside you. "What was that?" he whispers.

"Something outside."

"Should we go check it out?"

"No, let's stay in here for a while. It's probably nothing."

Then you hear another boom. And some kind of thudding sound, like a tree falling in the distance.

If a tree falls in the forest and barely makes a sound, is it worth heading into the darkness to investigate?

"Sounded like a tree hitting the ground," John Luke says.

You're still groggy from being awakened, but you're sure glad not to be talking to the groundhogs anymore. You wonder what you guys should do.

"Should we see what's going on?" John Luke asks. "That's why we're here, right?"

**Do you do the safe thing and stay inside?
Go to page 63.**

**Do you do the risky thing and check
out the sound? Go to page 205.**

C'MON, MAN!

IT'S DARK OUTSIDE, and you have no idea where the chain-saw dude is. But you're so close to the Jeep now, you go out in the open anyway.

Maybe you haven't watched enough movies in your lifetime.

Do you not understand that people who decide to be careless around chainsaw-wielding wackos end up in trouble?

Or do you not get that doing anything *other* than running far, far away from the crazy person is a bad idea?

But here you are, sneaking across the grass toward the Jeep. Peering around you to make sure the stranger with the chainsaw isn't nearby. You're crawling on all fours now to keep him from spotting you.

You don't think to actually look *in* the Jeep. Nah. Why would you do that?

You're too focused on your surroundings.

So when you reach the vehicle, you quickly open the back door, hoping to grab the rifle and dash into the woods again.

The first thing you notice in the back of the Jeep is a hockey mask. A very dirty hockey mask.

Then you spot a knife half-hidden under a blanket.

These two things are definitely *not* good to see. Like *ever*.

You gulp and say a quick prayer that God will protect you as you slowly lift a corner of the blanket.

Good thing there isn't a scary person underneath it. The chainsaw dude must have stashed his extra accessories here in John Luke's Jeep. C'mon now. What was he thinking?

Well, you're in way over your head at this point. Time to get John Luke and grab his keys from the cabin—as long as the chainsaw creeper isn't still hanging around there. You slip on the hockey mask as a disguise and pick up the knife for protection, then retrace your steps into the woods.

John Luke doesn't hear you come up behind him, so you tap him on the shoulder. "Hey, let's go!"

He turns before you remember you're still wearing the mask.

You've never seen anyone scream so loud or jump so high.

This mystery-solving stuff is more than you guys can take.

THE END

UH-OH

IT'S BEEN ABOUT HALF AN HOUR since you got into your sleeping bag. Everything's quiet outside except for the crackling of the fire. You're not sure if you're asleep or awake when you hear more strange sounds coming from the woods.

You open your eyes and confirm that John Luke is secure in his sleeping bag. He's definitely asleep.

The scraping sound of wood moves through the darkness. Of something tossing things around. Stepping on branches.

Then you hear a *scrape-scrape-scrape* that sounds like—

No.

But you're sure a creature is gnawing at some wood. Like a beaver . . .

Or an allibeaver.

Whatever it is, you know something's going on not too far from the fire.

It takes you a few moments to unzip your sleeping bag and climb out. Sure enough, John Luke is out cold. You keep hearing that tapping, chewing noise. *It's gotta be a beaver. A regular beaver.*

You pick up the flashlight and wonder whether you should grab your rifle too. Then you remember what John Luke said about cutting off the tail of the allibeaver. You know there's an ax you could pick up back at the cabin.

Which one will you take?

Do you choose the rifle? Go to page 47.

Do you choose the ax? Go to page 117.

DEATHTONE

BEFORE YOU GO INSIDE THE CABIN, you pause and tell John Luke to do the same.

"What?" he asks.

"Shhh. Just listen. It's so peaceful out here."

But no sooner have you spoken than you hear *something*— a barely audible something.

"Is that a phone?" you ask John Luke.

He nods. "It sounds like it."

It rings every few seconds.

"Where's it coming from?"

"I think the dining hall."

"They put one of those in there?"

"Not that I can remember."

It keeps ringing and you assume it's going to stop soon. But it doesn't.

The ringing continues on and on.

"I guess it doesn't have an answering machine," you say.

On about the fiftieth ring, you wonder if maybe one of you guys should go get it. "You think someone's trying to get ahold of us?"

John Luke checks his cell. "No, I got my phone here. And it has reception right now."

There's something eerie about the repeated rings of the phone. Over and over and over again. Not to mention that it might be hard to sleep.

"I can go get it," John Luke offers.

"Okay."

But you think about why Isaiah summoned you here and wonder why someone would be calling the camp.

Could be any number of weird reasons.

Do you play it safe and go to the dining hall with John Luke? Turn to page 181.

Do you decide there's nothing to worry about and let John Luke get the phone himself? Turn to page 79.

CHIEF STINKUM

YOU'RE BACK OUTSIDE, walking toward the lake, when curiosity gets the best of you.

You can't believe you're about to say this, but . . . "Tell me the story of Chief Stinkum."

"Dad tells it the best."

"You go ahead."

John Luke is still carrying the feather, still looking around for others as if they're clues. "There was once the Pungent tribe from the Great Reek Mountains."

You stop him. "Is this story all about bad smells?"

He laughs and keeps talking. "Their chief leader was a big man, a sweaty man, the kind of man who could bathe and still smell."

"Definitely sensing a smelly theme."

John Luke kicks a dead log as you follow him up a hill and into the woods. "He had four sons."

"Four, huh?"

"Yes, four. One was named Pompem. Another Stompem. Another was Cadagompem. And the final son was named Carl."

"Carl?"

John Luke nods. "Carl."

"Are you making this up as you go?" you ask him.

"Sorta. So anyway, this son named Carl, he always felt different. Maybe it's because his brothers had cool names and he was named Carl. But there was something else too. He didn't smell. All his other brothers were proud of the fact that they stank. They stank really, really bad. But not Carl. He could sweat in the sun all day but never start to smell."

"Is this a ghost story?"

"Yeah. Just wait. You'll see. This son, Carl, one day he decides he really wants to smell. So he tries to give himself gas. Like horrible gas. First he eats beans for breakfast. That works okay. Then he makes himself some stuffed boiled cabbage."

You abruptly stop walking again. "Wait a minute. When does this story take place?"

"They're a fairly modern tribe. Just work with me."

You nod for him to keep going.

"The stuffed boiled cabbage—oh, he's really starting to let it go now. But Chief Stinkum and Carl's brothers—Pompem,

Stompem, and Chompem—they don't care. They're not impressed."

"Think you got that third name messed up."

"So for dinner," John Luke continues in a loud voice, "Carl decides to buy a gigantic jar of pickled eggs that have been sitting in a gas station for who knows how long. Maybe years. He eats a dozen of them."

"When does the story get scary?" you ask as you arrive at the edge of Bluff Springs Lake.

"Right now. So the whole family's at a campfire—you know, 'cause you're tellin' the kids this story around a campfire—and the wind is strong. Carl is sitting there, and he can tell the wind is blowing in the direction of his three brothers and Chief Stinkum. As usual, they're laughing and ignoring him. So he waits for just the right moment."

John Luke pauses for a second, looking at you with a big grin. "Then *boom*. It happens. It's the loudest sound in the world. After that, the smell comes. And it's awful. People start running away from the fire. Others pass out. Some start crying. But Chief Stinkum doesn't move. He's tough. He's smelled worse. The floating cloudy mass somehow catches on fire, though, and that ends up shifting over to the chief, setting him on fire."

"A gas pocket sets him on fire?" you ask. "This really is scary. To listen to."

"Chief Stinkum runs down to the lake to douse the fire. But it's too late. He's gone. And later, at his funeral, the smell is still so strong that they can't have his body there."

"If Carl was my son, I might need to have some words with him."

"Now legend has it," John Luke says, "Chief Stinkum likes to haunt the kids at camp who smell the worst. He comes out from the lake and brings night terrors and bad breath. Whoever sees or is touched by Chief Stinkum will be stinky his whole life."

"Stinky his whole life, huh? That is one terrifying tale."

"My dad can really get going with the whole thing about Chief Stinkum coming back from the dead."

You smile and gaze over the lake. Several more feathers are floating on the surface.

"Did you put those there?" you ask John Luke.

He's staring at them in disbelief. "No way."

"You sure?"

"Yes, sir. But the camp counselors before us probably did. Having some fun with the kids. Maybe we should get them."

"Hmm. Maybe. But that is about the strangest campfire story I've ever heard. We could get a visit from Chief Stinkum tonight."

"I hope not."

Do you ignore the feathers but stay down by
the lake for a while? Go to page 51.

Do you let John Luke take the feathers
out of the lake? Go to page 17.

Do you head back to the cabins to pick
one to sleep in? Go to page 7.

CHOMP CHOMP CHOMP

SOMETIMES ONE SIMPLE CHOICE can change the course of your day.

And sometimes one quickly made decision can change the fate . . . *of the entire world.*

You tell John Luke to come with you into the woods. You have no reason to think that there's anything actually dangerous out there. If there's some kind of weird animal, then you'll find it and deal with it. On the other hand, if it's a bunch of kids playing some pranks on the campers—well, you'll deal with them too.

It's dark in the woods. The sky is clear and the moon is bright, but the trees are dense. Chirping crickets can be heard in every direction. Each step you take seems disruptive with the breaking of branches and the shuffling of boots over leaves and dirt.

"I think it came from this direction." You point that way.

You take a few more steps before you hear something strange. It's a different sound this time—a scratchy sort of noise.

"You hear that?" you ask.

"Yes, sir."

"It's like an animal's chewing on some wood," you say.

John Luke doesn't reply, but you bet you're both thinking the same thing.

The noise fills the air, and yep—you'd swear it sounds like a beaver chomping away on some wood.

You keep walking. There it is again.

The noise is coming from above us.

Then you hear another sound. This one is louder, wilder.

It's a low-rumbling bellow.

The chomping seems to be gone.

"You don't have a flashlight, do you?" you whisper to John Luke.

He reaches in his pocket for his cell phone. You're surprised that it's actually not a bad flashlight.

"Can that thing microwave some popcorn for me too?" you ask with a chuckle.

John Luke takes the lead, waving his glowing wand. The deep bass grumble can be heard again, this time directly above you—nearer than before. You look up, and it all happens before you can blink.

Something drops from the trees . . . landing on John Luke.

You hear screams.

You rush toward him, grab at the thing, and find it's some kind of—

No, it can't be.

But you don't think anymore as you rip at the tough leathery hide and try to get the long animal away from John Luke. It's an alligator from what you can feel and see, but then again . . .

It jumped out of a tree. An alligator literally hopped right out of a tree.

The gator suddenly gets on all four legs and starts to

You see its tail. Except it's like no alligator tail you've ever seen.

"Go on! Get!" you yell, and to your surprise it waddles away on its tiny legs.

Wait a minute.

That tail . . . it's long and round and . . .

You go to John Luke to avoid the craziness swirling around in your head.

"You okay, John Luke? That thing bite you?"

John Luke stands, and the first thing you notice is his eyes. They've darkened, yet they somehow seem to glow in the night. And then, right before your very eyes, he starts . . . changing.

I'm sleeping, and this is all in my mind. Those fried pickles have gotten to my brain.

John Luke's mouth and nose start to grow, to sprout out, to morph into something long. While his teeth—he's growing fangs. They're like alligator teeth.

It reminds you of those old horror movies where the man turns into a werewolf. Except this isn't a werewolf.

It's a weregator.

No, 'cause look at that thing sticking out of him—a tail, a beaver tail!

You back up, and you've never backed up from anything in your life.

But your grandson has turned into an . . . an . . .

He gets on all fours and runs into the woods.

You can feel your heart beating and your forehead sweating, and you know you've lost your mind.

Si's the one who's supposed to lose it—not me.

You snap out of it. Your grandson is an allibeaver, and you have to do something about it.

For a few seconds you can barely walk, your whole body shaking, your mind in shock. But then you start to jog. You chase him toward the cabins.

That's when you see the lights on the Jeep.

John Luke—no, he's an allibeaver now—is driving the vehicle.

The vehicle flies out of the camp and leaves you in darkness.

Do you return to the cabin and go back to bed since you're *surely* dreaming? Go to page 149.

Do you track down John Luke? Go to page 131.

LEAVING?

HOLD ON THERE . . . YOU'RE LEAVING?

You're no Phil Robertson. Phil would *never* leave someone screaming in the woods.

And if he did, John Luke would call Miss Kay and Willie to tell them there was an impostor with him.

No, no, no. You can't just leave.

Call the cops and go? Yes, it's certainly logical, but what does that have to do with anything?

Where's the adventurous spirit in you?

Where's the fight?

Oh, well. Time for bed. Let the cops solve the rest.

The adventure is over. Nighty-night.

Have some milk with your cookies.

THE WIMPY END

NOT SO SINISTER NOW

SOMETHING DOESN'T FEEL RIGHT about letting John Luke go alone. You realize it's gotten colder outside. Maybe it's just because you're no longer sitting by the campfire, but the wind has picked up and you're definitely feeling chilly. And you almost *never* feel chilly in West Monroe, Louisiana, this time of year.

John Luke enters the dining hall first and searches for the phone. Now that you're in here, you notice how high-pitched the ring is. It reminds you of the way your very first phone sounded. You can almost hear the clicking noise inside the phone, the ringer is so ancient.

You both spot the phone at the same time—sitting there on the floor by one of the tables. It's a black rotary, the kind where you have to actually turn the wheel with your finger to dial a number. No texting allowed on this bad boy! Maybe you should get one for John Luke.

He goes to pick up the still-jangling phone when you notice something odd.

It's not plugged in.

"John Luke," you say.

He turns toward you.

"Let me pick that up."

Maybe whoever's terrorizing the campers is playing a game right now with the two of you. You lean over and pick up the receiver.

"Who's calling?" you ask right away, without a greeting.

You hear laughter on the other end.

"Hello?"

More laughter. It's the sound of little girls.

Someone's prank calling.

"Hello?"

The laughter stops and you hear only heavy breathing. *Really* heavy breathing. As if the person on the line just ran a marathon.

"Who is this?" you ask.

"Hold on—let me catch my breath," a normal, average, not-creepy-at-all voice says.

So you wait a few seconds. "Still there?" you ask.

"Yes." The stranger clears his throat. Then coughs. Clears his throat again. "Hello," he says in a deeper, creepier voice.

You're about fed up. "Who is this calling?"

"Have you checked the children tonight?"

You glance at John Luke and roll your eyes. "Uh, look, fella. There's no children around here tonight."

"Exactly."

"You know you're calling a camp?"

There is a pause.

"That's right; you're calling a camp. Is this the same person who's been harassing campers the past week?"

The man on the other end clears his throat again. "Is this, uh, 37 Chestnut Lane?"

"No. Does it *sound* like 37 Chestnut Lane?"

"And you're not the babysitter?" he asks.

"Are you trying to be funny?"

Another pause, another slight clearing of the throat. Then the voice resumes its earlier tone—its very normal, not-so-sinister-sounding tone.

"You're not going to believe this, but I just made a big mistake. I think I dialed a nine when I really should have pushed an eight."

"We can trace calls," you threaten, even though you have no idea if this call can be traced.

"Look, buddy, it's all good. I'm just . . . It's just . . . it's nothing, really."

He hangs up, leaving you holding the receiver.

There's no dial tone or *eh-eh-eh* sound that comes on. It goes totally dead.

Dead silent.

"Who was that?" John Luke asks.

"A wrong number," you say, setting down the receiver. "Still, I think we should call the cops. Just to tell them."

"About what?"

"37 Chestnut Lane. Never hurts to be too careful. Let's use your cell phone this time, though."

You never thought you'd say those words.

But this feels like a solid lead on who might be behind the camp's mysterious happenings. That guy might act innocent, but only a fishy person could call a phone that's not plugged in.

Can the police track a call to an unplugged phone? Surely they can. And maybe they'll let you help interrogate this guy when they find him.

Mystery solved. You think.

THE END

PECULIAR MOSS

YOU'VE BEEN IN THE DIRECTOR'S CABIN for a few minutes when John Luke asks you about something weird in the corner, right by the doorway.

"Do you know what that is, Papaw?"

You rub your beard and stare at it for a moment. Then you get closer.

It looks like a green beach ball. But upon further inspection, you see that it's a clump of moss. You touch it and wrench your hand away immediately.

"That's real, all right," you say. "Burns to the touch."

"What's it doing here?"

"Maybe someone was usin' it as a foot warmer. Who knows?"

As you unroll your sleeping bag on one of the bottom bunk

beds (yep, even the director's cabin has bunks), you feel something strange on your fingertips. You look and see some of the moss stuck there.

"John Luke, I'll be right back."

You go into the bathroom to wash your hands, but for some reason the moss won't go away. In fact, as you scrub your hands together, the moss seems to be growing.

That's crazy. These old eyes are seein' things.

But by the time you turn off the water, both of your hands are covered in moss.

It's definitely growing.

"I think we have something peculiar happening right here," you call to John Luke as you return to the main room.

The ball of moss has been busy. Now it's covering most of the floor.

"John Luke?"

You find him on one of the top bunks, staring down at the floor.

"It's out of control," he says.

You show him your hands. Your fingers are no longer visible—they're just clumps of moss.

"Papaw!" John Luke shouts.

"I know. I think we need to get a little help. Whatever this moss happens to be, it's taking over my hands."

"And your head!"

You almost ask John Luke what he's talking about but

instead run back to the bathroom and glance in the mirror. Sure enough, somehow the moss got on your head. Parts of your hair are turning into moss. Your beard too.

"John Luke, we need to get out of here!" you shout, running back into the main room. He leaps off the bed and hurdles the multiplying moss.

The two of you escape from the cabin just as the moss overtakes the door and window. You stare in disbelief.

"Does this count as something we should report to Isaiah?" John Luke asks.

"Uh, yeah." The moss has stopped growing on your body, but your hands are still unrecognizable. "But first I'm gonna need to head home and get a haircut."

THE END

IT WAS ALL A . . . DREAM?

YOU WAKE UP in your own living room, more thankful for your favorite chair than ever before. The credits are rolling for some movie. It's playing scary music, so it must've been a horror flick. It's late, and most of the lights are turned off already.

You get out of the chair and stretch. Then you remember the dreams you were having.

Isaiah Bangs and a mysterious hitchhiker and Camp Ch-Yo-Ca . . .

And they were all just dreams.

But they felt so real.

How did I end up here?

You scratch your head, rub your beard, and squint at the clock. It's about two in the morning. Time to get back in your own bed.

Before heading there, you get yourself a glass of cold water. It tastes good on this muggy night.

You gaze out a window into the darkness.

Then you notice something right in front of you on the kitchen floor.

It's a mask. A white mask.

Where'd that come from?

You're not sure you want to know.

THE END

TWILIGHT ZONE

YOU FIND YOURSELF AT CAMP CH-YO-CA, but you can't really remember how you got here. You're alone and you're not sure what time it is.

What's happening?

It's sorta like a dream where you start the story midway through and aren't sure how you got there.

You're standing near the fenced-off swimming pool. You can hear voices coming from inside but can't quite tell who's talking. You try to open the gate, but it's locked. You call out, but nobody comes to open the door.

So you start walking around.

After a while of still not finding anybody (but now hearing the sounds of campers laughing and screaming in the distance), you decide to return home. But you can't find the Jeep. Come to think of it, you can't find John Luke either.

So you start walking down the dirt road leading to the main street that brought you here. Only tonight the dirt road keeps going and going. It doesn't end.

It brings you around to the back of the lake.

That's impossible. I just walked away from the camp.

So you do the whole thing again.

You walk over the hill and down a path through the woods until you get to the main camp area. Then you pass between the cabins, and farther on, you walk past the soccer field.

You keep going.

And going.

The dirt road winds around until you reach the edge . . .

Of the lake.

You're stuck here in Camp Ch-Yo-Ca. Still not sure how you got here. Still not sure how to get out.

Since you didn't follow any of the directions, you're caught in a never-ending episode of *The Twilight Zone*. You're the star and the host all in one.

Maybe you should start at the beginning. Think back . . .

Return to page 1.

ZODIE SIMS

"I DON'T KNOW who dropped that feather, but making up stories isn't helping anything. Let's keep looking for somebody around here."

So you do. But the camp is empty. All you and John Luke find are remnants of the summer: a child-size bow and arrow left outside, a log that's recently been painted bright colors, a towel abandoned on the grass, a journal.

You guys eventually give up and put your sleeping bags in cabin two—one of the boys' cabins—and you make a quick stop in the bathroom, dropping your shaving kit on the sink. Then the two of you head outside and proceed to build a campfire. Soon the fire is blazing, its flames waving up to the heavens.

"So tell me about this Zodie Sims." You can't help being a little curious about a name like that.

"It's just a ghost story that's been told over the years. Haven't you ever heard it?"

"I sure don't remember it."

"They say it's true."

"They say you can buy plots on the moon too."

He laughs, then sticks another log in the fire. "There was once this Camp Ch-Yo-Ca counselor named Zodie Sims. Everybody loved him. He was the best counselor who'd ever worked here. No one could imagine the place without him."

You nod and listen attentively to John Luke.

"One summer, a troubled kid came to camp. His name was Parker. Zodie took it on himself to help the kid out. He had Parker stay in his cabin, which was number six."

"I thought there were only five boys' cabins here."

"That's part of the story. Anyway, Parker kept getting into trouble. He'd sneak into the girls' cabins. Wander off and disappear. Stay up really late. They were on the verge of sending him home. But Zodie told them not to—that he'd really try harder to get through to the rebellious kid.

"One night, while everybody was asleep, a fire started in cabin six. Zodie got all the kids out of the cabin—or so he thought."

John Luke sticks a branch in the fire to move some of the red-hot logs around. The flames seem to go higher as he speaks again.

"With the cabin blazing in front of them, Zodie Sims

194

counts all the kids standing by him and realizes one is missing. He knows exactly who it is. So without even thinking, he darts back into the burning cabin."

John Luke pauses and stares at you. Then, in a slow, sad tone, he says, "Zodie Sims is never seen again. Neither is Parker."

"Well, that's not the happiest story I've ever heard."

"Ever since that fateful night, people have reported seeing Zodie Sims around the camp. Not haunting them, but looking for Parker. But the kid is nowhere to be found. The cycle never ends. Zodie keeps searching for Parker, trying to save him, but he never turns up."

"So Zodie Sims is sorta like Casper the friendly ghost."

"Yes," John Luke says. "He's not a malicious ghost."

"You've had some good fellowship with him, have you?" You have to smile.

"Zodie Sims is real," John Luke says in a serious voice that breaks into a laugh. "That's what I try to tell everybody, anyway. The kids love the story. There's a Zodie Sims Road around here. He shows up there all the time."

"I think if I died, I'd give up trying to find out where this bratty little kid happened to be," you say. "There'd be bigger fish to fry in the afterlife. I'd like to ask God a lot of questions."

"Zodie Sims is stuck here, don't you see? Since he can't find resolution on what happened to Parker—did he live or did he die?—Zodie Sims can't move on."

"So what *did* happen to Parker?"

"That's a good question. One that's fun to talk and speculate about."

"I bet Parker wasn't even in the cabin."

John Luke scratches his head. "A lot of kids who come to camp here think the same thing."

The wind blows the fire sideways, and you both get a mouthful of smoke.

"Maybe we'll see him tonight," you say in an eerie voice.

When you finally decide to go back to the cabin for bed, you discover something strange. Not only strange but a bit unsettling.

All the mattresses from the bunk beds—and there are about fifteen of them lined up in the cabin—are piled on top of each other on one side of the room. The beds have been moved together to allow the mattresses to be stacked like this.

"What happened here?" you ask.

"I don't know."

"It wasn't like this when we put our stuff in here."

John Luke nods. He looks a bit pale.

You let out a sigh. Something's definitely wrong.

Do you rearrange the furniture and get into
your bunk beds? Go to page 39.

Do you decide to sleep in another
cabin? Go to page 201.

WALKING WITH
JOHN LUKE

"ARE YOU SCARED, JOHN LUKE?" you ask your grandson as you enter the woods.

"No, sir."

"Good. There's no reason to be."

The screaming seems to have stopped for now, but a howl rings out, and it's not very far away from you.

"There's nothing to be frightened of," you say again. "Someone's probably playing a—"

There's the howl again, interrupting you. It sounds closer. Both of you stop.

"We should stay together, okay?" you remind him.

"Okay."

You take a few more steps before you hear it again. The joker must be nearby—unless this is actually a wolf.

"That was freaky," John Luke says.

"It's fine. Someone's just messin' with—"

Then you hear something falling in the woods—lots of things, like rain is pouring down ahead of you—but sticks and branches are falling, not rain.

The menacing howl comes again, long and loud.

You turn to John Luke. "Go!"

The two of you run back to the cabins, jump in the Jeep, and take off.

Whatever that was back there in the woods can stay in the woods.

It's one thing not to be fearful, to know God is in control, and to stand strong in moments of weakness, but it's also important to know when to use your plain, God-given good sense.

And right now, it's good sense to get out of here. To get *way* out of here.

Whatever you're leaving behind is gonna stay there for the cops and the authorities and those who look into things like that.

You're both feeling a little better since you're almost home by this point.

Then you hear a sound pierce the silence of the car.

"Ah-ooooooo."

THE END

THEY'RE HERE

YOU FIGURE YOU'LL CLEAN UP THE MESS tomorrow morning. Now you're tired and simply want to get some rest. So you and John Luke grab your stuff and go to a cabin next door.

A few minutes later you're lying in your sleeping bag in the darkness. Ready for slumberland.

But maybe half an hour later, you find you still can't sleep. Something about this cabin isn't right. There's more light here, for one. The moon is full and round tonight, and the bluish glow of it streams through the cabin windows. It's lighting up John Luke's face in the darkness. While many girls across the country might love this sight, you don't find it particularly wonderful.

It's a little *too* bright.

You close your eyes for another moment but open them

when you hear John Luke mumbling something. You notice that his eyes are open and the blanket is pulled up beneath his chin even though it's plenty warm in here.

"I see dead people," he whispers.

You move closer to see if he's trying to be funny. But he's just staring upward in some kind of weird, dreamlike trance.

"John Luke. Are you awake?"

He turns his head toward you, then lifts his hand. He balls his fingers up and begins to motion with his index finger.

"John Luke, stop this," you demand.

You know he's messing with you now, so you shake him, but his eyes don't connect with yours. He really must be in a weird daze. He's been known to sleepwalk now and then—at least he's staying in bed this time.

"John Luke, you have to wake up now."

He turns on his side as if he's going to sleep. You nudge him again but can't wake him.

"This isn't funny."

But you know he's not playing any game.

The moon still shines a spotlight on his bed. All you can do at this point is hope he wakes up normal in the morning. You settle back down in your sleeping bag.

At that moment John Luke pops up and looks at you. "Whatever you do, *don't* fall asleep."

Then he does exactly what he's telling you not to do: lies down and goes back to sleep.

There's no way you can follow his lead, though. Instead you stay up for most of the night, staring at the ceiling and glancing around from time to time. But you don't hear or see anything.

No ghosts or goblins or things that go bump in the night.

The mystery of the ghost of Camp Ch-Yo-Ca may never be solved. Until you realize . . .

What if it's John Luke? What if he's scaring the campers by sleepwalking over here in the middle of his dreams?

But no. That can't be.

There's no way.

You hear laughter.

Then John Luke's head pops up again and turns to you. "We all go a little mad sometimes," he says with a grin on his face.

His dimple glows in the moonlight.

The laughter comes again. It's loud. It's too much.

You jump out of bed and run outside. You've had enough.

Spending the night in John Luke's Jeep seems like the best plan. Tomorrow morning you can ask him what's going on.

If tomorrow morning ever comes . . .

THE NEVER-ENDING NIGHT

DIM DIM JOHN LUKE

YOU AND JOHN LUKE GO OUTSIDE to search the camp. He's right—that's the only reason you came in the first place. You head to the lake but don't find anything there. Then you circle back around the cabins and notice some more strange noises deep among the trees. You're familiar with a number of small trails throughout this forest, so you lead John Luke down the closest one, navigating with a flashlight.

"Think we're going to find anything?" John Luke whispers.

"Something's in these woods," you say. "I don't know what. But you heard it just like I did. Some kind of loud banging goin' on."

John Luke stays quiet.

"You're not nervous, are you?" you ask your grandson.

"No."

"You shouldn't be. Remember whose idea this was."

"But hearing this weird stuff is just kinda . . ."

"Just kinda what?"

"Weird," he says.

You keep walking with the flashlight pointed straight ahead, revealing the path and any other strange things you might come across.

"You know, when I was a kid, I hated the dark," you tell John Luke.

"No way."

"Oh, sure. And my father told me to picture the worst sort of thing I could imagine."

"Why?"

"Because then, if you never ran into it, you wouldn't have to worry about anything else."

"So what did you imagine?"

You laugh. "Oh, mine makes no sense. But for some reason, it terrified the life out of me. I was a boy—ten or eleven."

"What was it?"

"It's gonna sound crazy."

"What?"

You stop walking for a minute and let out a sigh. "A koala bear."

"A koala bear? Really?"

"Takes a proud man to admit he's terrified of a koala," you point out.

"Why? They're the sweetest animals in the world."

"Actually, no, they're not," you say. "They *look* like the sweetest animals in the world. But they're still *wild* animals. They have long, razor-sharp claws on both their hands and feet. And they're strong enough to cut you if they want to."

"A koala bear?" John Luke's still in disbelief.

"Opposable thumbs," you add. "Know what that means?"

"No, sir."

"They can grab you and hold down something they're trying to pry open all while squeezing their claws into your leg, chest, or whatever. So not only do they have sharp claws, but they'll grip on to you and it'll be painful."

"Are they mean?"

"I think I heard someone telling me a story about an angry koala bear when I was young," you say. "So that's what I thought of. I had nightmares about them. But ever since, I've never worried much about anything. Cause I've never encountered a koala bear."

You keep leading him into the woods.

"You ever been back this far?" you ask John Luke.

"I don't think so."

Both of you walk in silence for a few minutes.

"So what's the scariest thing you can think of?" you finally ask.

John Luke thinks for a minute before answering. "Cindy Rommel."

"Cindy Rommel. Who is that?"

He chuckles. "She's this girl I know from school. She just . . ."

"She likes you?"

"No. It's more than that."

"What? Why?"

"She *named* my dimple. Seriously. She has a name for my dimple."

"Is she not the sharpest crayon in the box, this Cindy Rommel?"

"No way."

"So what does she call your dimple?"

"She calls it her little Dim Dim. And that was just the start. She was sorta harassing me. She was an upperclassman."

"Her little Dim Dim?" you repeat. "Yeah, she sounds like a lot to handle."

You've just started to head up a hill when you hear something in front of you. It sounds like a low growl or bellow.

"Did you hear that?" you ask John Luke, stopping and shielding him.

"Yeah."

Then you hear this high-pitched laugh.

"And I heard *that* too," he says.

You've both come too far to turn back now.

"I don't know about this, John Luke."

"Just picture the worst," he tells you.

You keep walking hesitantly until you reach the top of the hill, where you scan your surroundings with the flashlight.

The good news is you no longer have to imagine the worst because it's standing directly in front of you.

The bad news is some pretty, blonde-haired girl with strange-looking eyes is standing there holding a koala bear in her hands.

You take a quick step back. "John Luke . . . is that—?"

"Yes," he says.

"Go!" you shout, and you both turn tail and run.

Nothing so un-scary has ever been this scary.

THE END

PRIMAL FEAR

A BOX OF MATCHES SPILLS OUT of the Jeep onto the ground. Then you smell the gasoline on John Luke.

That's when you notice the seat behind him. There's a can of gas resting there.

"John Luke," you begin.

"*No!*" he shouts in a voice that sounds a lot lower than it usually does. "It's in me! It's in me!"

You've never seen or heard John Luke acting like this.

"What are you talking about? What did you do?"

He shakes his head, waving at something that's not there, squinting his eyes. "The bats. They're back. The bats."

"Come on, talk to me now."

John Luke steps out of the Jeep. Behind him, the burning cabin fire rages on.

"What did you do, John Luke?" you say in a loud voice.

"A bat bit me," he announces. "When I was just a boy. I was only six! And you thought I might have gotten rabies, so they had to kill the bat. *They killed my little bat friend!*"

"What'd you have for dinner? Why are you acting like this?"

"The bat. It's the bat. Don't you see? Don't you understand? I'm not just a human anymore, Papaw Phil. Something happened. Something changed in me."

He's clearly delirious. "John Luke . . ."

"Don't you see? I have the blood of the bat flowing in me!"

"You have something flowing in you," you tell him. "But I think it's a bad fever."

Then John Luke is gone.

And you're left there stunned, your mouth open, without a clue to where he went.

Unsure what to do, you walk over to the burning cabin. Did John Luke really do this? And what in the world was he babbling about the bat for?

You hear something fluttering and see a bird fly by you.

Then it bites you, and you realize it's not a bird at all.

It's a bat.

And now so are you.

Batman's got nothing on me.

So much for solving this mystery.

To the Batcave!

THE END

FALLING SI

"PAPAW!"

You feel a hand on your shoulder. It's John Luke shaking you awake. You were searching the grounds of Camp Ch-Yo-Ca for so long that you lay down for a little rest, and you must have fallen asleep by the swimming pool.

You look up and notice how bright the stars are. You were dreaming that they were so close you could touch them. And that wasn't the only thing. For a second you thought you were Si on your way to Mars. What a crazy dream.

You remember what you were doing now. The camp director asked you to investigate strange events here. The mattresses in the cabin you were staying in were randomly stacked on top of each other while John Luke was telling you a ghost story at the campfire. The two of you went out in search of the culprit. The door to the fenced-in pool was open, and you thought the vandal might be in there, but no. He didn't even leave a message—nothing was floating on the surface of the still water, and the deck around the pool appeared normal.

"I think whoever was messing with us is gone," John Luke says.

"Yeah, maybe. Who knows."

Then you see something bright cascading through the sky.

"Look at that—you see that falling star, John Luke?"

He looks in the direction you're pointing, and you expect it to disappear. But it keeps getting brighter and brighter.

"Whoa, what is that?" John Luke asks.

It's getting bigger now, and it's coming right at you.

You hear an explosion, and fire rains from the sky. For a moment you're about to haul out of there with John Luke, but you wait.

The flames and bright glow have dispersed, and the object is now plummeting toward you with smoke streaming behind.

"A meteor is coming right at us!" John Luke screams, tearing away from you and heading for the woods.

You don't think it's a meteor. It looks like something else.

When the object is close enough to see, a parachute deploys, and you realize it's definitely not a falling chunk of rock. The parachute slows it down, and soon it glides right over you.

The oval-shaped object splashes directly into the pool in front of you. You stand to the side, ready to clear out of there at any second. Especially if Martians climb out of that thing.

But when the hatch opens, a familiar face peers up at you.

"You wanna help an old man out or something?"

It's Si, dressed in an astronaut suit. Somehow this doesn't surprise you. All you can do is shake your head. "*Where* in the world are you coming from?"

"Hey, listen, Jack. I just saw half the universe, and now I gotta go to the bathroom. Help me out of here."

When his capsule drifts over to your side of the pool, you grab his arm and pull him out. He climbs onto the pool deck, and you notice that his white spacesuit is covered in something. It looks like it could be blood.

"What's all that on your clothes?"

He shakes his head. "I'm tellin' you—I saw the dark side of the moon, that's what I saw. And it's pretty dark. It's too long of a story and if I don't go soon, I'm gonna explode."

You step aside, but Si stands motionless for a moment, staring into the distance. "It's good to be back on Earth," he says. "What are you doing here anyway? You look bored."

Before you can reply, Si wanders off to find a tree.

You simply want some sleep. You're too tired for another long, crazy story.

THE END

ZZZZZZZZZZ

FORTY YEARS AGO, you never would have fallen asleep. You wouldn't have done so twenty years ago, either. But somehow you end up fast asleep, and the only thing that wakes you up is the smell of smoke.

Smoke coming from a fire. A raging fire that's burning twenty yards from you.

The cabin. John Luke!

It's burning intensely, and you realize the cabin is already pretty far gone. You rush toward the building and know you shouldn't go in, but you have to. You don't see John Luke, and he could be unconscious inside for all you know. You call his name a couple times but don't hear any reply.

So you head in.

Thinking about Zodie Sims and Parker.

Inside, you find John Luke trying to douse the flames with

a bucket of water. You toss the bucket aside and grab his arm, forcing him to follow you. Both of you tear through the door you entered, flames licking you all over. You put a hand on John Luke's head as you exit the burning cabin.

Soon you're out, coughing and choking and kneeling on the ground.

"What happened?" John Luke gasps between coughs.

"I don't know. But whoever did this isn't trying to have fun. They almost killed you back there."

"I was about to leave when you came in. At first I thought I could put it out."

"Yeah, I know," you sigh. "But sometimes you just gotta tuck your tail and tear out of there."

You stay there on the grass for a while, coughing and choking and thanking God you're both okay as John Luke calls 911.

When the cops and the fire department finally arrive, an ambulance tries to take you to the hospital, but you refuse to get into it. You insist that John Luke go in for a checkup, though. You call his mother, Korie, who says she'll meet him there. While a medic looks you over, a cop comes by to update you: they found an empty can of gasoline in the woods. You proceed to tell him everything you know—what brought you and John Luke here, the strange things you experienced, everything.

Eventually you end up leaving when a worried Willie arrives to give you a ride.

It's only some time later—weeks, actually—when you remember Otis, the hitchhiker you picked up. You call the police and let them know. They thank you and take the info. But that's all.

That's the end of it. No more ghost sightings, no more weird noises in the woods. Otis must have moved on.

For now.

THE END

PEACE AND QUIET

"WE SHOULD PROBABLY KEEP GOING," you tell John Luke.

And yes, you do have places you need to be, but you're more concerned about picking up a crazy person with John Luke in the car. You know God is in control, but God also wants you to pay attention to your *good sense*. And your sense tells you picking up a stranger might not be the safest idea.

So you drive on.

You arrive at the camp and climb out of the Jeep. It's strange to see the place deserted. The cabin doors are closed. The picnic tables are empty. You hear the soothing sound of crickets.

"John Luke, are we the only ones here?"

"I think so."

The fire pit looks like it was just used a couple days ago.

"Which cabin should we put our stuff in?"

"Let's stay in the director's cabin," John Luke says. "It's a little nicer."

After unloading your sleeping bags and other belongings, you walk around the camp with John Luke.

"It's been a while since I was here," you tell him.

"You should come back sometime. The kids love it. Lots of great discussions around here."

You check out the rest of the cabins but don't find a soul. The gymnasium is silent and empty too.

● ● ●

Later that night, you're watching the fire you made an hour earlier die down. You've been talking to John Luke about lots of good things: where he wants to go to college, what he plans to study, why girls are so impossible to understand yet why they're amazing anyway. It's nice to have some one-on-one time with him.

"The camp's a lot different when it's quiet like this, right?" You poke the embers with a stick.

"Yeah."

You look up at the sky through an opening in the trees. The sight never gets old.

"See those stars, John Luke? Think about them. Think about who made them. Every single one of them—God simply waved his hands and the universe sat up. Kinda cool to think about, isn't it?"

"Yes, sir."

You remember the stranger you saw on the side of the road, waving his hand to try to get a lift. Where is he now?

Maybe we should've given the guy a ride.

You decide to put out the remaining embers and head toward the cabin for the night.

So far it's been a quiet and enjoyable evening.

You wonder why you had to come here in the first place.

You're pretty certain you'll sleep like a log and wake up tomorrow morning with nothing noteworthy to talk about. Unless you have some cool dreams.

Do you watch a little TV before bed? (The director's cabin has its perks.) Turn to page 111.

Do you stop and listen to the silence for a moment before turning in? Go to page 165.

Do you fall into a restful sleep? Turn to page 123.

Do you worry about the hitchhiker in your dreams? Turn to page 145.

THE HUNTER BECOMES
THE PREY

HUNTING REQUIRES PATIENCE. It requires waiting and watching. And honestly, if you were ever to be called something besides Duck Commander, it would be Patience Commander. You don't mind sitting still and just . . . being.

You've had a lot of practice at this. Being and waiting.

So that's what you do. And you have to do it for quite some time. An hour passes. At least you reckon it's an hour. Then another.

But you don't fall asleep. You watch the cabin, knowing someone's going to reveal himself. Knowing the mattresses didn't just happen to rearrange themselves. Knowing the toothpaste didn't put itself on the mirrors in the form of a disturbing message.

No, someone's doing this to mess with you.

And not a moment too soon, you spot the likely culprit.

Someone steps out of the woods and makes his way toward the cabin. The person is tall and wearing dark clothing and a stocking cap. He blends into the night pretty well, but you can still make out what he's carrying. It's some kind of can.

You don't wait any longer. It's the moment to act.

You stand and quickly approach the stranger from behind. As much as possible, you remain quiet and try not to be seen or heard.

Whoever it is, he's stopping near the front doorway and doing something with the can.

It's a gasoline can.

You don't have any more time for stealth. Time to deal with this.

You're running as fast as you can when you reach the creep and tackle him. He lands on his chest, and you can tell he gets the air knocked out of him. You dig a knee into his back and jerk an arm up.

Yeah, you might be over sixty, but you're not letting *anybody* mess with your family.

You can smell the can, and it turns out you were right. Gasoline.

The man is screaming now, and you see lights pop on inside the cabin. The door opens.

"John Luke, call the cops!" you shout. "Do it and stay inside."

The man struggles, but you stay on top of him and keep his

arm pinned back. He might be tall, but he's not particularly strong. You notice he has long hair and a beard. He also stinks. This is all strangely familiar.

Then you realize. It's the man you picked up earlier—the hitchhiker.

"What are you trying to do, huh?" you demand.

The man doesn't answer but keeps squirming.

John Luke opens the door again. "I called the cops."

"I've got this guy. Go take your rifle out of the Jeep. We need to keep an eye on this fella."

The cops arrive soon enough and put your prisoner in handcuffs. So far he's still said nothing to you. You've asked him to tell you about his plan, but not a word. And that's fine by you.

"Papaw Phil?" John Luke says after the police have taken the hitchhiker away. "I know my parents are going to freak out about this, but thanks."

"For what?"

"For saving my life."

You laugh. "Well, you're the one who held the gun. Maybe you ended up saving mine."

• • •

When the excitement is over, everybody learns the truth.

The hitchhiker you picked up wasn't any ordinary stranger. And he wasn't called Otis, either.

His name was Parker. Parker Adams.

Yes, he was that Parker.

The one who supposedly died in the awful fire at Camp Ch-Yo-Ca.

Turns out Parker lived. He ended up running away from the camp and from Louisiana and, as it happens, from all known sanity.

The cops tell you that Parker Adams had a strange fixation on the camp. Maybe because he ran off after setting fire to a cabin that killed a man years ago . . . a man named Zodie Sims.

Maybe that's also why he started harassing some of the kids around the camp, pretending to be a ghost.

• • •

A week later, you find yourself discussing the situation with John Luke. You're both sitting in your living room, John Luke on the couch across from you.

"Wow—I didn't even think the Zodie Sims thing really happened," he says. "I thought it was a camp legend. Just a ghost story."

"The only ghost I want to focus on is the holy one," you tell him.

But he has another question. "You think the ghost of Zodie Sims could have been haunting the camp?"

You pause for a moment, thinking. "I don't know about that. But I do know, as you've heard me say, that we eventually all get placed six feet deep into the ground. We all end up with a body that's as empty as a haunted house. We're all faced with the big questions of life and death."

You turn down the volume on the television.

"We're fortunate to know the truth. Zodie Sims—based on his actions, his sacrifice, it seems like he knew the truth too. That Jesus is the only way. But those who don't know get caught up in the mysteries and the bogeyman and the monsters behind the trees. They want to make these things up to help explain the unease they have about dying and where they're spending eternity. But the hope of eternal life with Jesus is a *fact*."

John Luke nods in agreement.

You give him a big grin. "But I do think that somewhere out there a scary-lookin' creature could be watching us. Waiting in the darkness. Preparing to jump out of the trees. But the joke's gonna be on us because he's gonna be as friendly as a little kitten."

THE END

SPIDEY SENSES

YOU'VE GOT BETTER THINGS TO DO than to keep looking for whatever kind of animal is making that weird noise.
You'd rather try to get some shut-eye.

The howling doesn't happen again, and you're pleased that,
for once, it doesn't take you a long time to fall back asleep.

• • •

When morning comes, you plan to investigate the source of
the noise that kept you up last night. But first you're going to
enjoy a cup of coffee and the bacon that Miss Kay is making
for you and John Luke.

The phone rings, and John Luke answers, then hands the
phone to you.

"Hello?"

"Phil, somethin' bad's happened." It's Isaiah. He sounds more worried than he did last night.

"What's goin' on?"

"The camp. There's been . . . I just got here and I don't—"

"Whoa, whoa. Slow down. Tell me what's wrong."

"It's covered in . . . I know this has to sound crazy, but it's covered in cobwebs."

You don't think you heard him right. "You say *cobwebs*? Like spiderwebs?"

"Yeah."

"What's covered in cobwebs?"

"*The entire camp.*"

You laugh. "What are you talking about?"

"You have to come see it for yourself."

"You're serious?"

"Dead serious. And even more freaked out than I was yesterday."

"Are you still around here? I thought you were going to a funeral."

"I'm heading out this morning. I swung by the camp, and then . . . then this. I don't even know who to call. I mean, what are the cops gonna do? And I have to get going. My flight's leaving soon."

"You go on, and John Luke and I will drive over there in a few minutes."

"Thanks, Phil," Isaiah says. Then he quickly adds, "Be careful."

The problems at the camp sound more urgent than whatever was in the woods last night.

•   •   •

You and John Luke arrive at the camp less than an hour after the phone call.

Isaiah was right.

It's unbelievable.

The first cobwebs you encounter are on the soccer field. They're so thick, the field seems to be covered in snow. But you know it's way too hot for snow. Plus, snow doesn't hang off goalposts like loose clothing.

"Is that for real?" John Luke says.

He's staring so hard the Jeep starts to drive toward a tree. You jerk the steering wheel straight.

"That is the creepiest thing I've ever seen," he whispers.

You pass a sign covered by what looks like a blanket. But of course it's actually a huge cobweb swaying slightly in the wind.

"Thousands of spiders must've done this," you say. "Hundreds of thousands of spiders."

"Where are they now?"

You're about to answer when you pull up to the cabins. They're all white. Every one of them. The webs are glistening sheets that glow in the sunlight.

It's the weirdest thing you've ever seen in your life. And you've seen some weird things.

The outdoor tables are also covered in white. You notice speckles of black on top of them.

"There are some of the spiders."

"I'm not getting out of the car," John Luke says. "Look at all of them."

You open the door. "Come on. They're just spiders. They're not buffalo." But you're beginning to have second thoughts.

The tree you're parked next to is smothered in spiderwebs. You swipe it to see how thick the webs are.

Dozens of spiders move down the tree.

You jerk your hand away and hop back in the Jeep. It takes you a minute to decide what to do.

Do you try to clean up some of the cobwebs yourself? Go to page 27.

Do you call for reinforcements fast? Go to page 83.

TRUE DETECTIVE

AS THE FIREMEN BEGIN PUTTING OUT THE BLAZE, you go straight over to the first police car that pulls up and tell the two uniformed officers that you'll be sitting at the picnic table if they need to talk to you.

Ten minutes later you watch a guy in a trench coat walk around the scene, talking to the other officers and looking for clues. He's wearing a Sherlock Holmes–type hat, and you half expect him to pull out a magnifying glass. Eventually he takes a call on his cell phone and walks in your direction after hanging up.

This trench coat dude must be a detective. You confirm this when you see he's wearing a badge that reads *Donny A. True Detective*. You snort when you first read it.

There's no way "True Detective" is his real last name. Robertson is a last name. True Detective is a made-up name that means you're not such a great detective after all.

Donny opens the notebook he's carrying and starts going through a page full of handwritten notes. "I'd appreciate it if you'd give me a full account of the events of this evening."

So you begin the story from the moment Isaiah entered your house. Donny cuts you off after you mention the hitchhiker.

"I suspected as much. My sources just confirmed the name of this drifter you encountered on the road: Nathan Fremont. Originally from Denver, Colorado. Spent some time in Florida and Georgia, then school in New York. Nathan Fremont's a wanted man in several parts of the country."

"For killin' people?" you ask.

"No. For making bad films. Really, really bad films."

"Really bad films?"

"So dumb they're inexcusable," the detective says. "He likes taking familiar horror movies and making them ridiculous. Basically he ends up insulting the directors of the original movies he's mocking. He's also been known to hypnotize some viewers of his films. When they're in the trance, he exchanges his film for another movie, and afterward the viewers awaken and think his movie was really great."

"He's actually done this?"

"Yes. He's wanted for questioning."

"So what do you think happened here?" you ask.

"I think he drugged you. You were both hallucinating when we found you."

"But everything that happened tonight—it's real."

The detective shakes his head. "He wanted you to *think* it was real. Your wallets were stolen. So was everything in your Jeep."

"How could he drug us?"

"The water in the camp," the man says. "Maybe he was starting to experiment last week and it resulted in some of the campers 'seeing things.'"

"What we saw was real."

"Really? Do you want to go on record about what you've experienced tonight?"

"I'd prefer never going on the record unless I'm talking about my faith."

The detective shuts his notebook and gives you a friendly smile. "I'm sure if you get tested out at the hospital, they'll be able to trace the toxins in your bloodstream. Your grandson's too."

"And that's it? Just like that. Everything explained?"

He nods, then thinks for a moment. "Some people in this life, Mr. Robertson—they like things spelled out. As in s-p-e-l-l-e-d out. But others . . . others like a little mystery. A little curiosity. A little lack of explanation. It boils down to who you are and what version you want to accept. The messy version? Well, you can go to whatever page is your fancy. But the neat, tidy version? Well, some only want to feel like the time they've spent has been worthwhile. They want a lesson and a pat on the back."

"I don't need either," you tell him.

"Okay. Then you two go home and forget about this. Forget that we ever showed up. Forget about ghosts and monsters. Forget everything and just move on. That's life, right? Strange things happen, and then you move on."

You watch him get into his car and leave. Then you look around the camp, knowing very soon it will again be full of life and love and prayer and faith.

Maybe a little mystery isn't such a bad thing after all.

THE END

THE SHADOWS THAT FOLLOW US

A Note from John Luke Robertson

THERE'S SOMETHING EXHILARATING about sitting in a theater and jumping in your seat at a scary part of the movie. Or walking through the dark forest and having your siblings pop out of nowhere and almost give you a heart attack. We hold our breath and freak out for a moment, sort of like when the roller-coaster ride takes that first inevitable drop.

But these are only temporary scares. They're fun and simple.

Life gives us daily opportunities for fear to be a real thing. Like the shadows that follow us on the sidewalk, we can't escape them. We can, however, *do* something about them.

Fears can be as small as worrying about a grade on a test or whether your friend will like the present you bought him. They can be big too. The anxiety of facing a bully nobody knows about. The dread of knowing your family is about to move to a new place.

The concern for a sick loved one. The terror of turning on the news and learning about the evil that's out there in this world.

The one solace we can take is that God promises he is there. That he will *always* be there.

I love the image that's described in Isaiah 41:13:

For I hold you by your right hand—
I, the Lord your God.
And I say to you,
"Don't be afraid. I am here to help you."

The God of this universe is right there, holding our hand. He's not too big to still be able to do that.

It reminds me of when I was young and I'd hold my father's or Papaw's hand. Their thick, rough hands reminded me I would be okay. They still do now.

It's fun writing about allibeavers and things that go bump in the night. When you're at camp, it's fun sharing spooky stories around a fire. But that's all they should be—fun. Like this book. It's great to laugh and even get a bit spooked from time to time.

God doesn't want us to carry our fears around, though. He wants us to know we don't have to be afraid. He really is walking right beside us, ready to protect and help us.